THE STORM BREAKER

VICTORIA KIMBLE

WALL CLOUD PRESS

For the Reid family.

I loved writing this story and thinking about Ashlyn.
I know she would have been fierce enough to stand up for
what is right.

CHAPTER 1

I BLINKED A FEW times and tried to focus on his words. His hair was so shaggy. Did they not have barbers in the City? And it was so gray. Not completely, but the brown that I remembered was clearly losing the battle.

I wished Trig was with me. He would have so much to say about the floral beach shirt and tattered flip flops. This guy looked like a cliche extra in an old beach movie. Trig and Penn would have enough material to roast him for an hour.

"You just look so much like Mella. I can hardly believe it's you. I mean, you're eight years old, right?" Dad asked.

Dad. I willed the tears that welled up in my eyes to go back to where they had come from. Why was I so surprised? I *knew* he was alive, when everyone else had written him off as dead ten years ago. But I couldn't get a word out, now that he was sitting next to me on the stone bench in the courtyard of City Hall.

It had taken some convincing to get Luca and Silas to let Dad go after he punched Matteo in the nose. Silas wouldn't let go until Matteo told him to. For the longest time, Luca stayed right by my side, as if he needed to protect me from this shaggy, tanned Florida retiree. Probably because the first words out of his mouth were, "why did you come?" Not exactly the welcome typically seen in long-lost family reunions. But as soon as they let him go, he jumped up and wrapped me in the warmest hug that instantly transported me back to the days when I was just a little girl, before he had gone missing.

Dad put his arm around me. "Ash, sweetie. It's okay."

I sniffed and buried my head in his shoulder. "No, it isn't. I mean, you're here. You're alive. Everyone said you were dead, but I never believed them."

He kissed my hair and laid his head on mine. "I never dreamed that I would get to see you again. But here you are." His voice broke on the last few words, and I lost it.

We cried together for a few minutes. I was only slightly aware that Luca, Cyra, Silas, and Matteo were on the other side of the courtyard, to give us space out of respect. Luca kept glancing over at me, worry written all over his face. I probably looked like a disaster. I never was a pretty crier.

I tried to pull myself together. I didn't have time for this. "Dad. We have to get out of here."

His eyes filled with sadness, and he pushed my hair out of my face. "I never expected you to be blonde."

I snorted a little. "I had to cut and dye it because Chip put out a nationwide search for me."

A muscle caught in his jaw. "Chip?"

"Yeah. He's dating Mom. He plans to marry her and run for President of the United States."

Dad was silent for a few moments as he stared at the ground. At last he took a deep breath and looked up, his eyes dull. "Well, I'm sure that's for the best."

My mouth dropped open, and I tried to process his words. Then I laughed. "Wait, what did you say?"

He gave a half-hearted shrug. "I'm so glad your mom is moving on. She deserves to be happy. And if Chip is in a position to run for president, he must be doing well. He'll take care of her. And Mella, and Trig, and Penn." He sighed and turned his face to the sun. "That's all I've ever wanted for my family."

I jumped up. "Are you kidding me right now? Are you seriously saying you are okay that your *wife* is going to marry someone else?"

He swallowed hard and gave me a look that adults sometimes give kids who don't understand things. "You have to trust me."

"Really? Why?"

"Because my job is to keep my family safe. And sometimes that means making hard decisions. Yes, I'm sad about this, but it keeps everyone safe, and that is the most important thing."

"How? How does letting another man marry your wife keep your family safe?"

He tugged me back down onto the bench. "Let me tell you the whole story."

I took a deep breath to calm myself down. This is why I had come. To find Dad, and to get the story of what happened to him. I needed to be mature and hear him out. I mean, it had been ten years. So much could happen in ten years.

"Okay. I want to hear."

"I served as Deputy Director of the United States Hurricane Agency for five years. During that time, I learned so much about Goliath that I wasn't able to share. I was legally bound to keep my mouth shut. I couldn't tell anyone, not even your mom."

"You mean, like the storm isn't real?"

"Oh, it's real. Didn't you see it when you came through?"

I rolled my eyes. "I mean, the storm isn't natural."

Dad sighed. "Right. I guess I can say it out loud in here. Yes, the storm isn't natural. Two teams of scientists worked together to create and capture Goliath, one inside the eye, and one on the outside. The team on the outside learned how to harvest energy, which made us energy independent for the first time in the history of the United States. So USHA was created to assist the team in the eye, so that we could maintain the energy harvest. And the care of the storm is handed down from director to director of USHA. As the deputy director, it was my job to learn how to maintain Goliath, in the event that the director became incapacitated."

He buried his head in his hands for a few minutes, looking ashamed. "I did the job for four years without question. I mean, the pay was great. I had four kids, and we lived in Colorado, so it didn't seem that big a deal to keep it going. But I was so fascinated by the science behind it that I dug deeper. And when I realized what I was a part of, I decided I had to stop it. We didn't have a lot of information about the tech inside the eye that kept it going, so someone was going to have to come to the eye, and I couldn't ask anyone else to take the risk. It was time for Goliath to downgrade to a Category Three like it did every ten years, so I planned a mission to come here and figure out how to turn it off."

None of this surprised me. Everyone had always told me he had a theory of how to stop the storm. I suppose nobody realized it wasn't a theory.

Dad's face darkened. "No one ever talked about how the government used the storm to bypass any eminent domain laws. I mean, they didn't have to buy up any of that land, because they just made it unsafe and forced people out. And so many people died. People have always died in hurricanes, but this was more than that. Since no one knew the storm wasn't going to go away, so many tried to ride it out. And they died."

I had never considered the deeper implications of what the storm did to others. It kind of made sense that Chip wanted to lead that kind of government. But that didn't change things.

"So, how is any of that relevant to the fact that you are okay if Mom marries someone else?"

He looked pained. "Chip was my best friend. He's always been a great guy, and I was aware he has always loved Livvy. I am sure he'll take good care of her."

Adrenaline surged through me, and I grabbed Dad's arm. "Are you kidding me? Great guy? He's a slimeball! He's the one who trapped you in here!"

Dad's eyebrows squished together. "No way. Chip did everything in his power to help my trip. He stayed back at headquarters to manage the fallout of what would happen with the Agency once I turned off the storm. But I couldn't contact him once I made it to the Eye, and clearly I didn't turn off the storm."

I shook my head. "No, Dad. Chip is the reason you're stuck here. He slashed your supplies in half the night before your mission. He withheld information about the shelters. He told me that you made choices that led to you losing your family, which totally means that he's the one responsible."

"Sweetie, you don't understand."

I clenched my fists. "No, *you* don't understand! Chip is the one who is in charge. He's using Goliath to get everything he wants, and his intentions are *not* honorable."

Dad tried to take my hand, but I kept my fist closed. "Honey, none of what you're saying makes sense. Listen. Let me finish my story. Once I got to the Eye, I met the Renwick family. They said they had a way to connect to USHA, and I went into a room that was set up for video chat. I dialed in, expecting to tell Chip I made it, and that I was ready to enact the next phase of our plan. But Chip didn't answer. Matteo did. Matteo, my other friend, who I thought was helping us this whole time. He said that if I turned off the storm, or tried to contact your mom, then he would get rid of all of you. Do you know they can create tornados?"

I rubbed my temples and nodded. "Yes. But Dad, it's not Matteo. It's Chip."

"No, it was Matteo. He said if Goliath ever dropped below a Category Two, then he'd unleash an F5 tornado on Castle Rock, and all of south Denver and you all would be wiped out. Of course I was shocked. I mean, he helped me plan the trip through the storm. But it was all a trap. To get me here, out of the way."

It all sounded so eerily identical to what I knew about Chip. Chip said he paved the way for me and the Storm Chasers to get in, so that I would be trapped in here. But one thing didn't add up.

"Dad. Stop. None of this is true. If it were, why would Matteo help us get in here? I mean, if he trapped you in here, why would he come with us?"

He scowled and shrugged. "I don't know. Probably to check on me."

"But if he's here, then he can't hurt Mom with a tornado, right? So we can go?"

"No, sweetie. I'm sorry, but no. We have to stay here."

Blood pounded in my ears. "But why? I don't get it."

"I know. But you will. I'll show you everything. You'll understand then."

I was used to the rage that built in my chest and overtook my body when I thought about Chip. But I was unprepared for that same feeling as I looked into my dad's face. Why did I think that finding him would be the answer to all of my problems?

I had spent the endless hours of our slow crawl through Goliath dreaming of what this moment would be like. I'd find Dad, who would be worn and haggard after his tireless efforts to find a way out of the eye. He would have spent every day of the last ten years working to find a vehicle that would be capable of getting him back north. Or maybe he would have worked twelve hours a day, trying to find a way to shut off the storm, only to be thwarted at every turn. Or the most likely scenario is that he was in some sort of prison camp, figuring out a way to survive.

But the truth was, he just got here and stayed. He didn't even try to get back to us. Mella had always told me he was dead, because if he was still alive, he would have found a way to get home. My stomach turned at the thought of telling her what really happened.

"Here's what I understand," I said through clenched teeth. "I understand you abandoned us. You should have at least tried to get home. But you didn't. You put up your feet and decided that the tropical life was the one for you, one without a wife and kids to tie you down."

Dad's face fell. "No. Ashlyn, that's not it at all. I had no choice."

I jumped up and backed away. "There is always a choice. You taught me that. And you also taught me that if I didn't like the choices, that I never had to settle. I could always find the right choice for me, even if it took some work. But I guess you were just lying to me."

He stood up and reached for me. "Ashlyn, wait."

I sidestepped his grasp. "No, thank you. I have to go." I turned and hurried away. I was too angry to even cry. I had no idea where to go, but I had to get out of the courtyard.

"Hey, where are you going?" Luca caught up with me and walked backward, trying to see my face.

I shook my head, unable to meet his eyes. I didn't want to see any of the Storm Chasers. They would never forgive me for dragging them down here to rescue a person who chose to stay.

Luca grabbed my arms and made me stop. "Ash. What's going on?"

I took a deep, shuddering breath. "He doesn't need to be rescued. We came here for nothing. And now we're trapped." Tears filled my eyes, blurring everything. "I'm so sorry, Luca. Your dad died for nothing."

He lowered his head to meet my gaze. "Hey. This wasn't for nothing. We found your dad. And we found a City in here, just like Dad said we would. We'll figure this out, okay?"

He pulled me into a hug, and I collapsed into his arms, sobs wracking my body. Luca held me as I cried, and his strong arms felt like home. He kept me in his arms when I stopped crying, his cheek on my head.

"I have no idea what to do now," I said, trying not to wipe my nose on his shirt.

He tightened his hug. "My dad always said to just do the next thing. And I have an idea what that is."

I leaned back and used my sleeve to take care of my nose, hoping he wouldn't notice. "What is it?"

"Let's talk to Matteo."

CHAPTER 2

Matteo already had the beginnings of two impressive shiners. It was a miracle Dad hadn't broken his nose with that punch. Silas had run back to the Turtle for our med kit and found an instant ice pack, which I'm sure helped with the pain, but would do nothing for the impending black eyes.

Cyra peppered Silas with a thousand questions about the ice packs when Luca and I walked up.

"So it's cold? Just like that?"

Silas gave her an odd look. "Yeah. It's basic chemistry. You break the stuff in the bag, and it creates cold."

She looked at the ice pack pressed to Matteo's face. "But, like, how cold is it?"

Matteo chuckled, which made his eyes water. "Do you want to touch it? You can, but I'm not taking it off my nose."

She looked like he had offered her a free puppy. She reached over slowly, as if the ice pack might leap out at her. She gave out a little squeal at the first touch, then pressed her entire hand on the outside. Matteo winced and leaned back.

Cyra blushed. "Sorry! That was so weird."

Silas looked amused. "Haven't you ever touched something cold before?"

She rolled her eyes. "Duh. But never anything like that. How is it supposed to help?"

"It helps with the pain and swelling. What do you put on injuries?"

"Just the spray that heals it."

I was intrigued. "Instantly?"

"Well, yeah. Don't you have that?"

Silas chuckled. "The only instant healthcare we have is this ice pack. Injuries need time to heal."

Cyra gave him a weird look. "Time? Who has time for that? Our Med Centers give people what they need, and everyone gets on with their life."

My mind clicked. "Oh yeah. You said something about no disease."

Her eyes widened, and her cheeks stained pink. "Oh, right. Um, sorry. I wasn't supposed to tell you that. It's one of the things we always heard that outsiders would come and steal from us."

For a brief second, I got mad all over again. I wanted to go home so badly, but there were so many things to learn about in the eye. First, I wanted to learn more about Weather Production and how they could produce tornados on demand and keep Goliath going for fifty years. Then there were these medical miracles that we had only dreamed about in the main states. I was being held hostage by the swirling death and destruction of Goliath, and by the intrigue of mysteries.

I folded my arms. "So. Matteo."

He stared at the ground. "Yeah."

"Is it true?"

"Is what true?"

I narrowed my eyes. "This is your chance to tell your story. I'm dying to see if it matches what Dad said."

Silas stepped in front of his brother, as if I might hit him, too. "Hang on a minute. What are you talking about?"

I shook my head. "This is Matteo's time to talk."

Matteo lowered himself to the ground. "Okay, but we're going to do this sitting, okay? My head aches, and if we're all seated, no one will be able to spring an attack on me."

Silas glared at him. "Why would anyone attack you?"

"I promise I'll tell you everything once everyone is sitting."

I rolled my eyes as we all sat on the ground in a circle, like it was story time at camp.

"Uh, where should I start?"

I leaned forward. "How about ten years ago?"

Silas looked back and forth between us. "Ten years?"

Matteo sighed and rubbed the back of his neck. "Okay. I guess I'll come out and say it. I've, uh, been working with Chip."

Cyra gasped. "Wait, that scum bag who is after Ashlyn?"

He nodded. "Look, you have to see it from my point of view. Chip has always taken care of me and my family. Silas, Mom and Dad have never needed anything. Did you notice that? And how about you? Did you ever have a problem getting donations to help you and the Storm Chasers survive?"

Silas' face had turned an unnatural shade of white. "What?"

Matteo shifted. "You know, those anonymous donations to help you and the key staff make your living? I couldn't have sent those in if it weren't for Chip."

Silas looked like he wanted to punch Matteo. "And why would Chip fund the Storm Chasers?"

"He didn't know! I mean, he never asked what I did with my money. It's none of his business. And it gave you something to do, and it kept you out of my business, so I figure it was money well spent."

"Start at the beginning," I growled.

Matteo shrunk back, as if shielding himself from another hit. "Okay, okay. So, back in the day, Chip, Jonah, and I all worked together at USHA. Jonah was Chip's right-hand man, and I was Jonah's. It was a good gig. The benefits and pay were off the charts. But Jonah started getting queasy about the storm. I mean, I understood his point, but by the time we got the jobs, all the damage had been done, right? So I didn't see any reason to upset the apple cart. But Jonah wouldn't let it go.

When Jonah planned the trip into Goliath, Chip asked to see me. He said he would give me a hefty annual bonus if I helped make sure that Jonah didn't make it. I told him I would try to talk Jonah down, but Chip thought he had passed the point of no return, and the only way to tie up that loose end was to make sure Jonah would never be able to say anything to anyone."

"So you plotted to kill him?" Cyra asked. "That's dark."

Matteo's eyes opened wide. "No way. Of course not. Jonah was my best friend. But the storm was bigger than any of us. So I got Chip to agree to send him to the eye. I mean, of course we knew about this place. Goliath was about to downgrade to a Category Three. So I told Jonah that I'd go with him to the eye to shut down the storm."

"Which was a lie, right?" I asked.

Matteo hung his head. "Yeah. I didn't want to go. So I faked the sinus infection, and of course Jonah insisted on going on the mission, because of the timing of the storm."

"And then you cut his supplies to make sure that he wouldn't reach the eye," I said.

He shook his head, wincing as the action aggravated his nose. "No, that wasn't me. Chip did that. Jonah and I also didn't know about the shelters. I found out about those years later. We always thought the supply convoys made it to the eye in a straight shot."

"You mean, you found out about the shelters after you threatened to wipe me, my family, and all of south Denver off the face of the map with an F5 tornado?"

Matteo groaned and put his head in his hands. "I promise that was a lie, too. I would never have done that. But when Jonah finally made it to the eye, we had to keep him from shutting everything down. He loved you guys more than anything, so it was the only leverage we had."

Luca cleared his throat. "This doesn't make any sense. I thought it took Jonah a few years to get to the eye."

Matteo nodded. "No one was more surprised than Chip and I when we got word that Jonah had crossed the eyewall. We really thought he was killed in the storm. We had no idea he found shelters, or that he would have found food and stuff. Although, now that I know about Ousley and other communities like that one, it makes more sense."

"There are more places like Ousley?" Silas asked.

"Who cares?" I exploded. "The point is, Matteo has been dirty this whole time. He tried to eliminate my dad. What I want to know is why he helped us get here. I mean, you *said* Chip was a slimy opportunist. You said USHA was dirty from the inside out. Was that all a lie just to get us to trust you?"

Matteo was silent.

"Talk," Silas said. "I want to know, too."

Matteo stared at the ground for a long time before looking up at me. "I was mostly telling the truth. Chip really is a slimy opportunist. I didn't lie about that. But you do what you gotta do, right? I told Chip I would help get you here, to get you out of the way. And then when Silas came, I thought that maybe he and I could just live here in the eye, too. I'm tired of working for Chip. Living inside Goliath really takes a toll, and I'm ready to retire. I figured we could all make it here and you would all realize it's not a bad place to be."

Luca leaned forward, his face inches from Matteo's. "But not everyone made it, did they? Chip's goons killed my dad."

Matteo scooted back. "That wasn't supposed to happen. I don't know why Chip sent in the military. Except, probably so he could say that he did everything he could to get Ashlyn back."

That checked out. It was exactly the kind of thing Chip would do to keep up the appearance of having nothing to do with any of this.

I wasn't sure how to respond to any of this. On one hand, it meant that everything Dad told me was true. He stayed because our family had been threatened, and he wanted to keep us safe.

On the other hand, it meant that Chip had been actively destroying my family for ten years.

I had one more question. "Did you know Chip was dating my mom? I mean, before we found you in Traxler."

Matteo stared at the sky for a long moment before nodding.

I stood up and walked away from the group, rubbing my temples. I had some answers. But none of them solved my problem.

I hated I had trusted him. I guess he was true to his word when he said he'd help me find Dad. He just left out the minor part that he was the one responsible for trapping Dad in here. He was just as culpable at breaking apart my family as Chip. And for what, money?

I kept walking. I had no idea where anything was. I could get lost. But it didn't matter. The City was completely enclosed by Goliath, so I'd hit the edge eventually. And also, I had nowhere to go. So it didn't matter where I went.

The movement felt great. I had been cramped in a Turtle for a week, then cramped in the shelters whenever we stopped. If I had had a pedometer on, it would have shown less than five hundred steps a day. Walking in the fresh air with a light breeze was pleasant. It was warmer than I had imagined. I laughed a little as I realized I was still wearing my rain jumpsuit. I unzipped the top part and pulled my arms out, thankful I had worn a T-shirt that day. I let the sun hit my bare arms as I crested a small rise. I froze, staring out at the eyewall of Hurricane Goliath a few miles away. The dark swirling clouds looked like one of those random scenery images on the wall screens at the dentist's office.

I heard footsteps behind me, but didn't feel like turning around. I had nothing to say to anyone. Not even Luca.

But it wasn't Luca. It was Silas.

"Ashlyn, I'm so sorry." The anguish in his voice caused me to turn around. Silas' eyes were red, and a muscle in his jaw twitched. "I had no idea that Matteo did any of this. He never said. But I never questioned him. I always thought he was just my supportive big brother who was my partner in the Storm Chasers. I never even imagined he could do something like this."

My heart broke for him. I tried to picture how I would react if Trig told me he had done something this horrible. Would I still love him? I guess I would, in that you-love-your-family way, but it would definitely change things between us.

"It's not your fault."

Silas choked back a sob. "I realize he makes his own choices, but I should have seen this coming. We didn't have a lot of money growing up. Mom and Dad always gave us everything we needed, but only what we needed. No one needs new tech or trips or meals out. I should have known something was up when Mom and Dad started going on those vacations in the first-class cars on the trains. I figured they had more money because they didn't have to take care of us anymore. Not that their fun money came from Matteo's dirty scheme."

I reached out and touched his arm. "I don't blame you. I'm serious."

He took a deep breath. "Thanks for that. So how can I make this up to you?"

I let out a little laugh. "There's nothing to make up, because you did nothing wrong. But I guess the next thing is figuring out how to get out of here. Chip said Goliath is already up to almost a Category Six. We'll never make it, not even in the Turtle."

Silas stood next to me and stared at Goliath's eyewall. "We'll have to figure out how to shut it down."

"And how are we going to do that?"

He shrugged. "If they are keeping it going, then we can turn it off. And Chip trapped us in here with nothing else to do. I mean, I've got all the time in the world. How about you?"

My brain started spinning. He was right. What else was I going to do here? "It's not like we can just walk in to wherever and hit a switch."

Silas grinned. "No. Of course not. But listen, I've learned a few things over the past few years as head of the Storm Chasers."

I laughed. "Like how to break into USHA?"

"Something like that. But that's, like, Step Ten of our plan."

"And what's Step One?"

"Rebranding."

I stared at him. "What do you mean?"

"Well, we don't have any more storms to chase, do we? So the Storm Chasers need to be rebranded to the Storm Breakers."

That sent me into a fit of laughter. I'm sure it wasn't that funny, but the combination of the events over the past few hours caught up with me. "Silas, that is so corny."

He shrugged. "But it's accurate, right?"

I stopped laughing and looked at him with a huge grin. "Yes."

"Then welcome to the team, Storm Breaker." He stuck out his hand, and I shook it, still giggling at the ridiculousness of this little ceremony.

Silas turned and headed back to the group. "Come on. Step Two is to find a place for a meeting."

I hurried to catch up. Our job wasn't done.

CHAPTER 3

There was a weird standoff going on in the courtyard when Silas and I got back. Dad was on the far end of one side and Matteo was on the other. Luca and Cyra stood in the center, their heads swiveling back and forth between the two, as if ready to jump into action and tackle someone.

I headed straight for Luca. "What's going on?"

He folded his arms. "Your dad came out and looked like he was going to jump Matteo again. As much as I wanted him to, I thought it would be best if everyone stayed on their side of the yard."

Silas nodded. "Very wise."

I looked around at our group of four; Luca, Cyra, Silas, and me. The beautiful weather was a stark contrast to the tragedy of the situation. We had left Denver with a group of nine. Tyler died in Macon. Sybil took his body back to Murfressboro. Hugh, Ginger, Jack, and Miri were lost when an attack tornado dropped on us about twenty miles outside of the eye.

We found Matteo in Traxler, and Cyra in Zuber. But Matteo obviously didn't count. And this was Cyra's home. She wasn't really one of us.

Luca put his arm around me. "How's it going, Booker?"

I sighed. "I miss Hugh."

He raised an eyebrow. "You miss *Hugh*?"

"And Ginger, and Miri, and Jack. And your dad. And Sybil. There were so many of us, and now there's not."

Luca's muscles tightened at the mention of his dad. "Yeah."

Silas cleared his throat. "Uh, Cyra? Do you have any idea where we're going to stay? Are there any empty houses?"

She shrugged. "I guess I'll have to ask Adele."

Adele. I wished I could live my whole life without ever seeing her again. She was practically in Chip's lap, doing whatever he asked to keep the storm going. But she *was* in charge of the City. Which meant she was going to be in charge of our stay here.

"Will you find her and ask? We, ah, don't know what to do next," Silas said.

Cyra looked surprised. "Oh. But aren't we leaving? Remember? You promised that if I brought you here, you'd take me when you leave?" Her voice had taken on the edge that a little kid gets when they are promised ice cream, but are afraid they aren't going to get it.

"I remember. But we're not leaving yet. We'll need a place to stay for a bit."

Cyra huffed out one of her famous sighs. "Fine. I'll go ask."

She shuffled away, and Silas tightened up our group of three as soon as she was out of earshot.

Luca raised an eyebrow. "Could you be any more obvious, trying to get rid of her?"

Silas shrugged. "Well, we do need to know where we're going to stay. It'll be easier to have our first meeting that way."

"First meeting?"

I rolled my eyes and smiled. "First meeting of the Storm Breakers. That's what he's calling us now."

Luca tipped his head back and laughed. "Are you serious, man? That is so corny. What are you, a teenage girl, always needing to name your club?"

Silas set his jaw in defiance. "Names help us keep our goals in focus."

I let Luca have his moment and waited until he finished laughing. "You don't want Cyra to be a part of us?"

Silas shrugged. "I haven't learned enough about her yet. Yes, she was trying to get away, but I can't get a read about how she'll feel about our plan to turn off the storm."

Luca widened his eyes. "We have a plan to turn off the storm?"

Silas nodded. "Well, not a full plan. But that's the goal. I mean, we have to, if we want to leave."

"But what about the Turtles? Can't we just use them to leave?"

I shook my head. "First, they're too slow. It's not like we can make a fast getaway, and Chip would have Adele sick her dumb tornados on us. Plus, Dad said Goliath is almost a Category Six already."

Silas nodded. "They were only designed to withstand a max of a Category Three. Or else we could have taken them in at any time. There's a reason we had to wait until Goliath died down."

Luca sighed and laced his fingers through mine. Warmth filled my belly as I gripped his hand and hugged his arm. He looked down at me. "Well, Booker? What's the next thing?"

"The next thing is letting go of my daughter." Dad's voice broke in and we jumped apart. It was an automatic reaction, ingrained in me from my youth to jump at the sound of a parent's voice. I hadn't heard Dad's voice in ten years, but the timbre and echo of his voice still had the same effect.

Rage bloomed in my belly. I stepped back, grabbed Luca's hand, and glared at Dad. "I'm eighteen now. I'm pretty sure you have no right to give us any steps."

"I'm your father."

I narrowed my eyes. "Well, sounds like you have no right to that anymore, either. Not after willingly giving it up to stay here in La-la-land."

Dad gave me a pleading look. "Ash. Please. I told you why."

Luca cleared his throat and let go of me. "Let's start over. I'm Luca Denzio. It's nice to meet you, Mr. Booker. I've heard a lot about you." He held out his hand.

Dad stared at it for a few seconds, then swallowed hard and shook it. "It's nice to meet you, too. Thank you for bringing my daughter to me." His voice caught on those last few words.

Silas sighed and stuck out his hand. "I'm Silas Chapman. Matteo's brother. We've never met, but I've heard a lot about you, too. And I want to say that I'm so sorry about what Matteo has done to you. I promise I had no idea."

Dad gripped his hand in a warm handshake. "Ah, Silas. I remember Matteo talking about his wild baby brother. His stories of you guys growing up sounded a lot like my Trig and Penn."

I wanted to snap that he had no idea how Trig and Penn were. But he was right. I had thought that several times over the last two days since Matteo joined us. Watching Silas and Matteo together felt like getting a glimpse of Trig and Penn in their forties. Hopefully, they'd be married with kids of their own, rather than still living together in that tiny apartment in Castle Pines.

Dad let go of Silas' hand and stuffed his own hands in the pockets of his khaki shorts. "I don't hold anything Matteo did against you. I'm not even sure I hold it against him."

My mouth dropped open. "Are you kidding me? Which is it, Dad? Did Matteo steal your family from you, or did you just give up on us? You can't have it both ways."

Dad shook his head. "I knew Matteo wasn't as well off as us. And I'm aware of what USHA was offering to keep quiet about everything. I mean, I thought Matteo had more integrity than that, and I was disappointed when I saw his face on that screen when I made it to the eye. But I've had seven years to think about it. I get why he took the money."

Luca's dimple appeared as a small smile grew on his face. "So that was a 'hey, man, I get why you did what you did' punch in the nose?"

Dad looked over Silas' shoulder at Matteo, who sat under a tree with the ice pack still pressed to his face. "Okay, maybe I wasn't as healed as I thought I was when I saw him in person. But I'm good now. I mean, I'm going to get Adele to find him a place to live and work on the other side of the City. But whatever. Live and let live."

This weird, hippie version of my dad was freaking me out. I remember he had a good sense of humor and was the 'nicer' parent, letting us kids get away with stuff that Mom would never have if she had been there. But this was a whole different level.

"Live and let live, even if that means your wife marries another man while she's still married to you?"

Dad sighed. "Ashlyn. What is it going to take for you to trust me? To understand?"

"Nothing. I will never understand. Because you don't seem to understand the kind of man Chip is."

Silas broke in. "I can solve this." He turned and cupped his hands around his mouth. "Matteo, get over here!"

Matteo stood looking like a whipped dog. He approached the group with cautious steps. "What?"

Silas grabbed him by the shirt. "Tell Jonah about Chip."

Matteo kept the ice pack on his nose, as if that would prevent Dad from punching him again. "What about him?"

I threw my hands in the air. "That he is just as responsible for Dad's failed mission as you are."

Matteo looked back and forth between Dad and Silas, as if what we were asking him was a trap.

Silas let go of his shirt. "Come on. We're trying to help you out here. Jonah thinks it was all you. And, of course, own up to what you did. But tell him how Chip was involved. It's important."

Matteo took a step back and straightened his shoulders. "Chip and I have worked together this whole time. He's the one who asked me to make sure you never made it out of the storm. And when you made it to the eye, he told me he'd double my pay if I told you I was the one who could unleash the tornado. It seemed impossible you'd survive, so I didn't see any reason not to take the payout and do what he said."

Dad's face turned white. "Are you kidding me? You *and* Chip did this?"

To his credit, Matteo looked miserable. "Yes. I'm totally responsible. I'm so sorry, man."

"See?" I jumped in. "It was Chip. What Matteo did was disgusting, but Chip let him take the fall for it, but was just as guilty. And you want Mom to marry that guy?"

Dad swallowed and took a step back. "I, I can't believe this." He stumbled over to a bench under a cluster of palm trees and sank down. His chest heaved with rapid, shallow breaths, and he wrung his hands for a few seconds before covering his face.

I watched him, helpless. I hated that my emotions were ping-ponging all over the place, bouncing between anger at him for not trying to get home to us and horrified sorrow for him at what it is like to get this news for the first time.

I started to go over to him, but Silas put his hand on my arm.

"Just give him a few minutes," he murmured. "Let him process."

My eyes filled with tears, and Luca pulled me into a hug. Matteo seemed to know it was time for him to retreat to his corner of the courtyard again and he slinked away.

"I don't know what the next thing to do is," I said.

Luca tightened his arms. "You want to know what I think we should do next?"

I nodded.

"Find something to eat."

I pushed away from him in surprise. Then I laughed. "Yeah. I could eat."

Silas looked around the courtyard. "I hope Cyra comes back soon. The sooner we find out where we can camp out, the sooner we can start on our plans of how to shut this place down."

A tiny flicker of hope sprang alive in my belly. Chip had forgotten one thing: I was not my dad. I did not accept that he could just threaten whoever he wanted, and I would not just roll over and let him have his own way. Chip had given me the gift of time to figure out how to stop him, and I planned to use it.

Cyra entered the courtyard, rolling her eyes harder than I had ever seen. A man and a woman trailed two steps behind her as she marched over to us.

"Guys, this is my mom and dad, Gwen and Xander." She sounded as excited as someone announcing they were going to watch a software update. "They think they need to be within touching distance of me at all times."

Gwen rolled her eyes, and I almost laughed out loud. Apparently, Cyra came by that little mannerism honestly. "Cyra, you *ran away*. You literally drove into a deadly storm. I don't trust your judgment, and it makes sense that I want eyes on you."

Cyra folded her arms and huffed. "But I didn't die, did I? And I came back, didn't I?"

Gwen gave a tight smile and looped her arm through Cyra's. "No, you didn't, and yes, you did. And so we're going to start from scratch. But for a few minutes, I'm going to stay close and hug my baby, okay?"

I could tell that Cyra was trying to hide a smile. "Whatever. Look, this is Silas, Luca, and Ashlyn. Oh, and that dirt bag over there is Matteo. They all need a place to stay."

Gwen and Xander looked at each other in surprise, then at us with curious expressions. "You're from the storm?"

Silas laughed. "No, we're from the mainland. We just came through the storm to get here."

That made Xander look nervous. "Why did you come? And how did you get through Goliath?"

Luca grinned. "Well, it wasn't easy. We came to find Ashlyn's dad."

Cyra shrugged. "Oh, yeah. This is Jonah's daughter."

Gwen gasped and dropped Cyra's arm. "Jonah?"

Dad crossed over to our group, eyeing me to see how I would react. After watching how Gwen was with Cyra, I understood Dad a little better. I gave him a small smile, and he stepped into the group.

"Yes, this is my youngest daughter, Ashlyn." He put his arm around my shoulder, and I gave Cyra's parents an embarrassed grin.

Gwen covered her mouth. "Well, you're all coming home with me. I need the whole story."

Xander didn't look as enthusiastic, but he gave a nod, and turned and headed out of the courtyard.

Silas sighed, then called out for Matteo to follow. I frowned, and Silas turned to me with an apology in his eyes. "Sorry. He has to come with us. I'm responsible for him."

Dad set his mouth and nodded. "We'll figure out something."

"Come on!" Gwen called over her shoulder. "I wasn't prepared for guests, but I always have cheese for sandwiches."

My stomach gave a loud growl as we picked up the pace.

Luca grabbed my hand and grinned. "I don't hate that cheese sandwiches are our next thing."

I laughed and followed the group out of the courtyard. For the first time, it hit me that we made it. I was safe, and I had found my dad. I had no idea how we were going to get back home, but I figured a cheese sandwich in my belly might help us figure it out.

Chapter 4

If I closed my eyes, I could pretend I was on the Senior Trip I voted for, instead of lying on a kitschy floral padded lounge chair in Cyra's backyard. The delicious warmth of the sun, the sound of the palm fronds brushing together on the slight breeze, and the smell of salty sea water combined with hibiscus all made me believe I could be some place else. Our senior class had the option of going to southern California or Seattle. I voted for warmth. But most of my class voted for gray skies.

I mostly didn't blame them. Everyone who grows up in Colorado, where there is sunshine three hundred days out of the year, romanticizes what life would be like in the dreary Pacific northwest. I wasn't too mad when the Seattle trip had won out. But I had figured that by April, most of us would be tired of cool, mild temperatures and ready to work on our tans. Plus, I wanted to see the Disneyland Ghost Town. The old, famous amusement park had closed when Mom was a kid, and some enterprising organization turned it into this fantastic ghost town. I loved historical things like that.

The brief contentment of the moment dissolved when I thought about Dasha. My best friend. She was probably on the bullet train back to Denver from Seattle right then.

I tried to swallow around the lump that had grown in my throat and hoped she had had fun with Gretchen and Rosalie, our two other friends. I had hurt her when I told her I wasn't going with her to Seattle, but to Florida with the Storm Chasers instead. I wished I could contact her somehow. She would get home that evening. Would she tell Mom what I had done?

Part of me hoped so. If she did, Chip would have to admit a few things. Or, at least, he would finally have to lie. It made me sick that he truly had been able to tell my mom the truth this whole time, while hiding his role in Dad's disappearance.

But part of me hoped she wouldn't. I didn't want her to put Mom in danger. I know Mom was going to ask her, but I wanted her to just say that she hadn't seen me since the light rail station the day the class left.

I didn't open my eyes when I heard someone drag another chair close to mine. Opening my eyes meant I had to face the world, and I was tired.

"How's that cheese sandwich treating you?"

I smiled at the sound of Luca's voice. "Like it's the boss of me now, and it wants me to sleep here for a few weeks."

"A few weeks?"

I turned my head and cracked open an eye. He perched on the edge of his chair, as if about to run away.

"Is that too long?"

"Well, I was hoping you'd want to go for a walk."

The warmth in his voice kicked up the delicious feeling of butterflies in my stomach. A walk away from the prying eyes of everyone around us sounded way better than a nap in the sun.

I jumped up and grinned. "Yes. Let's go. Should we tell someone?"

Luca rolled his eyes. "I think that sometimes you forget you're an adult now."

My cheeks warmed. "Yeah. Sorry. It's a casualty of being the youngest."

"You didn't act like this on the trip down here."

I shrugged. "I guess reconnecting with my dad caused me to slip into my old ways. I've spent my whole life asking for permission to do things, and only the last week making my own decisions. Give me a break."

Luca grinned. "Do what you gotta do to relax, okay?"

As much as I wanted to just go, I felt compelled to stick my head in Cyra's house and announce to Dad, Silas, and Cyra's parents that Luca and I were leaving. Dad opened his mouth like he was going to question me, but Silas caught his eye and shook his head. Dad snapped his mouth shut and nodded.

I marched around the house to the front yard, where Luca waited. "I didn't ask; I *told* them I was going."

Luca grabbed my hand. "Good. Now, get in the Turtle."

I stopped. "Why?"

He looked around, then leaned closer and lowered his voice. "We should go. Now."

My heart pounded, and I glanced over my shoulder back at the house, as if Dad or Silas were watching.

"We'll never get away."

"Why not?"

"You heard. Goliath is a Category Six now. The Turtle can't survive that."

Luca folded his arms. "I think they're bluffing."

I shook my head. "Dad wouldn't lie about that."

"So, he's not lying. I bet he doesn't know. Ash, he's afraid. He's not questioning things because he's worried about your family. I don't agree with it, but I think that's what's going on here."

My heart warmed as Luca defended my dad. Or it could have been the fact that I had been lying in the sun for an hour. Or maybe it was the hope that had sparked in my chest.

I came to the eye because I knew in my heart Dad was alive, and I was right. I still believed Chip needed to be stopped. I took a deep breath in through my nose and straightened my shoulders. It was silly of me to think that all I had to do was make it to the eye. Of course, this was only the first part. Now that I had my proof that Dad was alive, I needed to finish the job. The job was always getting him home. And since he seemed to think that he needed to stay in order to keep us safe, then I was going to have to stop Chip on my own. But I couldn't do that from inside the eye.

I took a step toward Luca and lowered my voice, a force of habit after our week of having zero privacy and listening ears so close by. "What's the plan? "

"Let's leave. Right now. Get in the Turtle and drive back the way we came. They won't expect it."

He was right. This was the perfect time. They already expected us to go on a walk, so no one would expect to see us for a while. And the Turtles were practically silent, since the wind charged them. Surely spending seven days in the winds of Hurricane Goliath meant we still had enough juice to make it back to the storm.

I couldn't resist one more glance at the house as Luca and I climbed in the Turtle. Everything was calm.

Our drive out of the City felt anticlimactic. No one followed. There wasn't a soul on this side of town. I thought we'd see a lot more people once Adele lifted the Shelter Drill, but I had no idea where everyone was. Based on my conversations with Chip and Adele, I expected there to be some sort of security on the road to the tunnel that lead out of the eye. What else were those military goons that were guarding City Hall supposed to do now, but make sure we stayed put where Chip wanted us? But the only exciting thing was the sight of Goliath.

No wonder no one in the eye ever tried to leave. The dark clouds of the eyewall roiled and billowed like thick smoke. I had never seen clouds that looked like that. They looked unnatural. But I shouldn't have been surprised. Since Goliath wasn't natural, why should its clouds be?

Luca slowed to a stop before entering the tunnel that would lead straight back into Goliath's wrath. "You ready?"

My throat caught. Was I being impulsive? I just found Dad, and I was about to leave him less than six hours later.

But I had so much information. Dad's life, Chip's involvement, and even USHA's involvement. I had to get back to the mainland in order to expose everything.

"Yes. But even if I'm not, we have to go if we want to make it back to the Zuber shelter before dark."

I pulled out a tech pad to check on Goliath's status as we drove through the tunnel. My stomach sank. "Luca, they weren't bluffing about Goliath."

"How can you tell?"

"This says the sustained wind speeds are already at two hundred miles per hour."

He tightened his grip on the wheel. "How long have they been like that?"

I pressed a few buttons. "I don't know. But I've never seen the winds this high in all my life."

He chuckled. "Only you would have the historical data memorized."

I socked him in the shoulder. "What, you didn't have any hobbies as a kid?"

"Yeah. Regular ones. Like VR games."

I scoffed. "Nerd."

"Hey. I only played the physical ones, where you punch bad guys. None of those world-building games."

I smiled at the mental image of Luca as a little kid wearing VR goggles and punching at imaginary bad guys.

The smile on my face disappeared the second we exited the tunnel, and Luca swore. He slammed on the brakes and the Turtle lurched to a stop.

Six massive tornados sat on the other side of the laser pillars, blocking the road and miles on either side. It took me a moment to realize that they weren't moving; they just stood there.

"How is that possible?" I asked. It was a stupid question, after what I had learned about Goliath and what I had seen from the other tornados that Cyra's friend Pax had dropped on us while trying to get to the eye. But once again, I was witnessing a brand-new weather phenomenon. Never in the history of ever had tornados stayed in one place. Somehow, the R and D department had figured out how to make them stationary.

I was so busy staring at the tornados that I almost missed the person running toward our Turtle. They looked like a young teen boy, but it was hard to say because he was covered from head to toe in a rain jumpsuit. He ripped off his goggles as he ran towards, waving one arm wildly.

I gasped. "Is that Jack?"

Without discussing anything, both Luca and I jumped out of the Turtle and ran to meet Jack in the middle of the road. In truth, the last time we had seen him was that morning, when we left the shelter. But so much had happened in the past six hours that it seemed like they went missing years ago.

I gasped and covered my mouth as soon as we were close enough to get a good look at him. His normally goofy, boyish face was marred by dried blood crusted over his eyebrow, and his left eye was almost swollen shut. He cradled one arm close to his chest, and my stomach turned at the sight of his wrist turned in an unnatural position.

Jack managed a grin. "Hey, guys."

Tears filled my eyes. "Hey."

Luca swallowed hard. "What happened? I mean, is everyone okay?"

A sob caught in Jack's throat. "Uh, not really. That jerk of a tornado carried us a few miles away and then dumped us in a field. Don't be mad, but Miri and I weren't wearing our seatbelts."

Luca's face turned pale. "Where's Miri?"

"She's in the Turtle, but she's not in good shape. We were tossed around with the crates like we were in a snow globe. She hit her back on the corner of one of the crates, and she can't move her legs."

Luca took off running, and I chased after him. Ginger jumped out of the Turtle as soon as we got close. She grabbed me in a hug while Luca raced on to the Turtle.

"Did you make it?" she asked.

"Yeah. We just left to go back to the mainland."

Ginger shook her head. "You can't. The storm has intensified faster than I've ever seen. We barely made it here. Hugh pushed us as fast as the Turtle would go, and then those tornados dropped. We stopped here to figure out if we should go through the tunnel."

I glanced over her shoulder. "How bad is Miri?"

Her face turned grave. "Pretty bad. We haven't moved her much. We hoped to get somewhere where we settle for a bit."

For the first time, I took a good look around. Wind speeds reached roughly thirty miles per hour, while the sun remained hidden behind clouds that seemed to hold the tornados in position. To the northwest stood the wall of tornados. There seemed to be nothing on either side. And behind us rose the massive hill with the gaping tunnel. The towering pillars that supported the lasers pointed at Goliath's eyewall were solid, windowless structures. I didn't see how they could be used for shelter.

I sighed. "We can all go back through the tunnel."

Ginger looked surprised. "We can? I mean, it's not guarded?"

"No. They really do trust the storm to keep people out. The tunnel is a little over a mile, and then it's perfectly pleasant weather. It's creepy."

Ginger tapped on her tech pad. "I can't get the tech to update. Right now, it looks like the eye is a dead zone."

Luca jumped out of the Turtle and ran back to us. "We've got to do something. Miri was talking, but then she passed out."

Ginger's eyes filled with worry. "She's in a lot of pain. I don't have anything that can touch it."

My heart sank. All the hope I had of getting back to the mainland fizzled away. "I bet they can help her in the Eye. Cyra told us they have instant healing. She freaked out about an ice pack, because they have nothing like that. Just instant sprays that heal everything on contact."

Relief washed over Luca's face. "Oh yeah. I forgot about that. Yeah, let's go."

I looked at Ginger, who checked her pad one more time. "Okay. I guess we don't have any other option. Did the rest of your group make it? Silas and Matteo?"

I let out a mirthless laugh. "Yep, we all made it. We have a lot to tell you. Just follow us. You'll see."

CHAPTER 5

MELLA USED TO TELL me I needed to learn how to handle disappointment better. I always hated that. Did she want me to smile and say thank you when things didn't go my way?

The radio crackled to life. "Booker, Luca wants to know if you can go faster."

I gritted my teeth as I gripped the wheel. Driving the Turtle was as scary as I expected. I had never driven a vehicle this long before.

Ginger patted my arm. "You're doing great." She pressed the button on the radio. "She's doing what she can. Tell them to hang in there."

"You got it," Hugh said. "I'm just trying to keep you both happy."

Not only was I driving something scary, but my stomach was in knots over the way Luca insisted on riding with Miri back to Cyra's house. He wouldn't even drive her Turtle; he wanted to ride in the back with her to make sure she didn't shift around. Ginger said she would do that, since she had been since Miri got injured. But Luca insisted.

So Hugh drove the battered Turtle, and I drove ours. I guess I could have gotten Ginger to drive, but I felt like I had to prove myself. It was dumb, but I wanted to prove to

Luca that I was capable of handling things, like driving the Turtle and his long-standing friendship with Miri.

Ginger gasped as we exited the tunnel into the bright sunshine. I didn't blame her; the sun was shocking after a week under the dark clouds of Goliath. She pressed herself against the windows as I drove through the vacant town to Cyra's house.

"Are there people here?" she asked.

I gave a shrug. "That's what they say. To be honest, we haven't seen them yet. They were all in a shelter drill when we came into the City this morning."

She clutched my arm. "I'm such a dolt. I didn't even ask. Did you find your dad?"

I let out a little laugh. "Yeah. He's here. Apparently he's just been hanging out here for the past seven years, because Chip got Matteo to tell him that if he tried to contact us or get out, that they'd flatten Denver and the entire surrounding metro area with an F5 tornado."

"Wait, Matteo? Our Matteo? I mean, Silas' Matteo?"

Heat flooded my cheeks. "Yeah. He's a real prince. He's been working for Chip this whole time. He helped trap my dad in the eye, and he told Chip he'd get me here safely to get me out of the way."

Ginger was silent for the next few minutes. It was hard to tell if she was in shock over the tropical paradise we were driving through, or over the revelation of Matteo's betrayal. "So I take it that Goliath's sudden increase wasn't an accident."

I turned onto Cyra's street. "Another 'Welcome to the Eye' present from Chip. Or Adele. Adele is the mayor here, and she's been doing Chip's bidding. Apparently, USHA keeps everyone in here supplied and comfortable, in exchange for their help in maintaining Goliath. So, yeah, they can control the strength of the storm."

I checked the mirror for Hugh's Turtle as I pulled to a stop in front of Cyra's house.

"Who's that?" Ginger asked.

Adele stood on Cyra's front porch, waving as if we were long-lost relatives who finally made it after a long road trip.

A sour taste filled my mouth. "That's Adele. She is our personal welcoming committee."

Adele glided out to meet us as we exited the Turtles. "There you are! And you found your friends. How wonderful. Hi everyone. I'm Adele, mayor of this beautiful City."

Hugh, Jack, and Ginger looked at me, as if I could translate what she was saying. Her greeting was so odd.

"What are you doing here?" I asked.

Adele gave a sparkling smile. "We monitor our borders, so we saw when you took your Turtle back through the tunnel. I had them turn down the wind so you could take a nice look around when you got to the other side. I figured you'd be back sooner than later, so I thought it'd save time if I met you here. I admit I wasn't expecting your friends, but no matter. I'm glad they're safe."

Luca hurried out of the Turtle and ran up to Adele. "Miri needs help. She's hurt. Really bad."

Adele pasted on a look of concern. It looked like it was a face she had practiced in the mirror. "Oh my. What happened?"

I clenched my fists. "You did this to her. You and your stupid guard tornados. They tossed that Turtle before we got here. And now Jack's arm is broken and Miri can't move her legs."

Adele stuck out her lip. "Goodness. I'm so sorry that happened. But you can't blame us. You're the ones who insisted on coming all the way down here, even though a sane person would have stayed away."

Luca took a step toward her. "She needs help. Now."

Adele stood her ground and smiled up at him. "Well, now, why should we use our resources on an outsider? I mean, I know it looks like we live in a dream, but we have limited resources. We have to prioritize them for those who live here and contribute to our society."

Ginger's mouth dropped open. "What are you saying? You aren't going to help?"

Adele lifted one shoulder in a shrug. "I'm saying that our healthcare is for contributing members of our society. Now, the good news is, you all can become contributing members of our society. If you do, then we can help."

"So, what do we need to do? Like, sign something?" I asked.

Adele flashed a grin. "Don't be silly. All you have to do is promise me you won't try to leave, and that you'll commit to the jobs we give you."

Ginger let out a huff. "So, we are prisoners."

Adele's laughter rang out. "Oh, you all are so dramatic. Do you want help for your friend or not?"

Ginger looked around at our group. "Can we have a minute to talk about this?"

"No!" Luca broke in. "We'll do it. We'll do whatever you want. Just help Miri. Please."

My heart twisted as I looked at the anguish on his face. He wasn't the only one thinking back to only a few days ago when his dad lay on the floor of the carport in a pool of his own blood. After what Cyra had told us, I couldn't help but wonder if Tyler would have survived if we had had the medical care of this City.

Adele looked at me. "Is that what you all agree to? You'll stay and join our little community, and you won't try to leave again?"

Luca turned to me with pleading eyes. "Ashlyn?"

I grabbed his hand. "Of course. Whatever it takes."

Adele clapped her hands. "Oh, good. Let me go make a call. Our med team will be here in just a few minutes. Don't worry; there's never been an injury we haven't been able to correct."

"What about a severed foot?" Jack asked, still cradling his arm. Thankfully, Adele ignored him and went into Cyra's house, and Ginger gave him a death stare.

Luca's shoulders drop and a sob choked his voice. "Thank you."

I squeezed his hand. "Don't worry. If everything that Cyra told us was true, she'll be fine."

Hugh folded his arms. "Were you lying when you said we'd live here and get jobs?"

I gave him a wry smile. "Maybe. I mean, we are trapped here right now. So we're going to need something to do while we figure out our next move."

Jack rubbed the back of his neck with his unbraced hand. "But you said we wouldn't try to leave."

"But I never said we wouldn't try to shut down the storm."

Relief washed over Hugh's face as the door to Cyra's house banged open, and Silas came rushing out.

Ginger ran to him. They embraced in a hug and starting kissing in a way that made us all equally uncomfortable and unable to look away.

"What am I watching?" Jack asked.

"How long has that been going on?" I asked.

Hugh rolled his eyes and gathered us together to walk away and give them some privacy. "They've been together for two years. They just don't flaunt it like you young kids."

My cheeks heated as I looked at Luca. Worry etched his face. Not even Silas and Ginger's passionate reunion seemed to take his mind off of Miri.

A gentle whooping siren filled the air as a med bus glided down the street. Everything about this City was relaxed, even their emergency services. It wasn't that they weren't taking it seriously; it seemed more like they were just purposeful and confident, which gave them the ability to be calm. Luca ran to meet them at the Turtle, and four people in white coveralls moved to assess the situation. They gently pushed him out of the way, and two women climbed inside the Turtle. The men standing outside returned to the med van and brought back a stretcher that hovered on its own above the ground. They glided it to the Turtle as two women got out. The men climbed inside, and the women pushed the stretcher into the Turtle. Within seconds, the men were back outside, pushing Miri toward the med van. The stretcher hovered above the ground without any wheels and glided easily, as if drawn back to the van.

I gasped and ran to the group. "Was it safe to move her?"

One of the women put her hand on my arm. "We stabilized her first. Don't worry. We can help, but only back at the med center. Our healing sprays can't fix spines, but we have the healing chamber for that."

I wanted to argue. I had no idea what they were doing to her. I had never heard of any of these things before. But Luca put his hand on my arm, and I knew what he was thinking. We had no other choice but to trust them.

"Can I go with her?" Luca asked.

The woman eyed him with suspicion. "No. Adele only said that one of you needed attention."

"No, two people need attention. Jack broke his arm."

The woman glanced at Jack's bent wrist and clucked her tongue. "Oh, dear. Here, we can fix that right now." She ran to the van and hurried back with what looked like a basic arm brace. Jack winced as she guided it onto his arm and then pressed a button. Jack's wince melted into awe.

"It's cold. And that feels much better."

She grinned. "Leave that on until we bring your friend back. Don't move it. Your bone will be healed by the time we return."

A muscle jumped in Luca's cheek, and for a second I thought he looked disappointed that Miri wasn't going to have one of us go with her. "Okay. Can we come see her later?"

The woman gave him an amused grin. "Sweetie, she'll be back in less than an hour. But only if we leave now. The sooner we go, the less time she'll need in the chamber. Okay?"

Luca nodded, and the med team jumped in their van and the van slipped back up the street.

By the time we got back up to the house, Ginger and Silas had finished their kissing session. Ginger looked slightly red, and Silas had a grip on her hand that looked like he wasn't planning on letting go anytime soon. I cocked an eyebrow at them. "Well?"

Silas shrugged. "It was none of your business. But I thought I lost her."

Ginger couldn't stop the grin on her face. "Sorry, guys. I hate PDA."

Jack laughed. "We just had a near-death experience. If I had someone to suck face with, you better believe that's what I'd be doing right now."

For the first time since we found the rest of the team, Luca grinned. "Well, Cyra's right inside, Jack."

Jack's face turned beat-red. "Uh, I meant someone like Ginger. I mean, if I was Silas, and Cyra was Ginger, and we had been together for a while—"

We all laughed as Jack flubbed out his words. When he finally settled down, Silas scowled at Luca and me.

"You guys have got to stop trying to run."

Luca shrugged. "Hey, if we didn't, we might not have found these guys."

I sighed. "Don't worry. We can't. They've locked us in here good. There were six massive tornados on the other side of the pillars outside the tunnel."

Hugh folded his arms. "I think you should know that Ashlyn and Luca just committed us to living here and contributing to their society."

I shot him a look. "It was in exchange for help for Miri. What would you have done?"

He twisted his mouth. "The same, I guess."

Silas motioned for us to tighten our circle and lowered his voice. "You should know that Adele showed up about thirty minutes after you left for your 'walk.' She told your dad that if he couldn't keep you in line, then her arrangement with him couldn't be guaranteed."

My mouth dropped open. "What arrangement?"

Silas shrugged. "But don't worry. We'll figure this out. I guess we have to wait for our assignments. One step at a time."

The door to Cyra's house opened, and Adele poked her head out. "Come on, friends. I think I have housing assignments all ready for you. Come inside so we can chat about it." She waved and winked, then went back inside without waiting to see if we would do what she asked.

Ginger wrinkled her nose. "I can't decide if she's trying to be diplomatic, or if she's patronizing us. She expects to be obeyed, doesn't she?"

Luca nodded. "Cyra told us she's in charge because her dad passed it on to her. They don't vote for their leaders. So they've got a whole monarchy thing going on."

I folded my arms. "She's pretty high and mighty for someone who is playing Chip's lapdog. I don't know what he promised her, but she's very proud that we're here and she's in charge of us."

Silas narrowed his eyes. "For now, we're going to play along. I figure if we do what they say, maybe we'll get access to Weather Production. Or their communications, at the least."

Dad met us at the door as we entered the house. His face looked tired.

"Ashlyn, please don't leave like that."

A rock formed in my stomach. "I'm sorry. I thought I could get back out. And I didn't want you to talk me out of it."

He sighed and pulled me into a hug. "I know this is hard. I promise to give you the space you need to process and accept it. But you'll see. We can make this work."

"You're just going to let Chip win?" I whispered.

His arms tightened. "Sometimes it's not a matter of whether we let things happen. They just do. And our job is to figure out how to adapt."

I sighed and pulled away to follow the group into Adele's stupid meeting. I just wanted to talk to my mom. That was the real goal, now. Tell Mom the truth about everything. As soon as the truth was out, Chip would lose all of his power.

CHAPTER 6

My dad lived in a pool house in Gwen and Xander's backyard.

I stared around the room in the fading light of the evening. It was the size of the tiny shelter in Zuber where we found Cyra. Basically, a standalone studio apartment.

Dad cleared his throat. "Ah, you can have the bed. I'll take the couch. I promise I keep the bathroom clean. Your mom was always a stickler for that, and it's something I've kept up all these years."

I asked the first question that popped into my mind. "Does Adele know where you live?" I couldn't get the memory of the twinkle in Adele's eye when she said that I was to stay with Dad, since that would be the most fair.

He chuckled. "Well, yes. Although, I bet the pool house at the mayor's mansion is much bigger than this, so she might not realize that not all pool houses have actual bedrooms."

I dropped my bag. "Dad, I can't stay here."

He put his arm around my shoulders. "I'll help you find a better place close by. You're old enough. Most kids are assigned their own housing when they turn eighteen. But please stay for a little while, okay? I want you to tell me about everyone and everything."

I was still mad at him. But a deeper part of me needed my dad. So I nodded. He grinned and hugged me tight, then moved to clear some things off of the tiny table.

"I don't spend much time here. I've always spent most of my time with Gwen and Xander. Gwen has been a real gem to keep me fed."

I snorted. "Remember that one time you tried to cook us dinner, when Mom was on the Western Slope taking care of Gramma? I will never forget the flash cooker shouting at you to stop pushing so many buttons. I've never heard it do that again."

Dad grinned. "I was always more of an order dinner kind of guy. It's worse here. They don't have pod meals or flash cookers. They cook things the way they used to back in the old days, with ingredients and pots and pans. They've never even heard of pod meals here."

I sat on the bed, surprised at how comfortable it was. "What's the deal with this place? It looks like something out of our history videos, but they have the craziest medical advances. So are they in the past, or in the future?"

Dad stopped tidying and turned. "It's both. I can't wait to show you around. My theory is they do so many things the old way because they were hyper-focused on the weather production and medical tech."

"So, have they told you the whole story? Like, how did they get involved with Goliath? Because I've seen the pillars. Clearly, they've been there this whole time."

Dad sat on the couch and patted the seat next to him. "They're still kind of tight-lipped about everything. But here's what I have figured out. The storm started here, with the Renwick family. About sixty years ago, Adele's grandfather and a team of scientists discovered how to generate hurricanes using drones and lasers to heat the temperature of the waters of the Gulf of America."

I sat on the couch and tried to think. "I remember that from class. There were a few years where the southeastern states got pummeled with back-to-back hurricanes for a few seasons."

Dad nodded. "Of course, everyone focused on climate change and political unrest followed. So the government created the United States Hurricane Agency to focus on the problem.

By this time, Ashton Renwick had figured out how to control the direction and duration of the hurricanes, but he still managed to make them look random. The head of USHA was a woman named Gabrielle Moreno. She had been appointed through some backdoor, shady dealings with lobbyists who had something over the president. Of course, no one was aware she had been working with Renwick for years on the hurricane project. She had been the creator of the energy harvesting technology, which she conveniently slowly released to the public while she was head of USHA. Her job was to distract the country with the advances in energy independence, while Renwick created this City, where they were able to run programs and experiments outside of government oversight.

Finally, Renwick managed to harness one massive hurricane over the Orlando area, and Gabrielle used the resources of USHA to supply the City with whatever they needed. And I do mean whatever. Renwick's son Brady was in politics and had been pushing for a lot of socialized programs, but of course, at that time, the population wasn't going for it. Once they realized they could cut off the City from everything else, Brady figured that everyone on the inside would 'choose' his programs, because they had no other choice."

I shook my head. "And people went for that?"

"You'd be surprised at what people let the government get away with when they're scared. First, they hunkered down to shelter from the hurricane. Then, when they realized it wasn't going away, they became afraid of what would happen to them since they were cut off from the rest of the world. The conditions were perfect for a takeover."

"Okay, but what happened when they realized the storm wasn't natural?"

Dad sighed and leaned back. "The best I can tell is, by the time any of them realized it, they loved what they had. They had already made remarkable advances in medicine, and the leadership drilled into them that the rest of the world wanted to take it from them. And now it's been long enough that they take it for granted. Most people don't care; they just go about their lives. You'll see that a general attitude of Not My Worry around here. If it doesn't directly affect them, they don't ask questions."

"Hey! Jonah! Open up!"

I jumped at the sound of Cyra banging on the screen door and shouting, as if we weren't sitting a few feet away.

An amused smile appeared on Dad's face. "Come in, Cyra."

Cyra looked furious as she threw open the door. "Why didn't you ever tell me?"

Dad folded his arms and leaned back, as if settling in for a lovely chat. "Tell you what?"

She rolled her eyes. "Anything about the storm? You just made me feel bad about myself, and like running away was the only option I had."

I wanted to hear this too. Everything Cyra had told me about Dad did not sound like the person I grew up with. She described a mean-spirited bully. I raised my eyebrows and waited for him to speak.

Dad sobered up and leaned forward. "Cyra, I'm sorry. I've always looked at you like you were, well, Ashlyn. I wanted better for you than being stuck here for the rest of your life. You're a free-spirit who shouldn't be cooped up in four thousand square miles."

"And so you bullied me so I would leave?"

He looked ashamed. "I admit, it wasn't my best option. But you've always been pretty stubborn. And I knew that the window when Goliath was weakened was so short. If I had just told you to go, would you have?"

Cyra looked defiant for about two seconds, and then her face fell. "No, I guess not. I would have called you one of the Kooks."

That got my attention. "Who are the Kooks?"

Dad gave a small grin. "They're a small group of people who live on the other side of the City who have been trying for years to expose the storm. Most people think they are crazy."

Cyra nodded. "Yeah, because they're, like, a thousand years old."

"They're original residents. They were teens when the storm hit, so they've seen it all. But most people ignore them, because they like their lives."

I threw my hands up. "Why didn't you go to them? They could've helped you with getting out."

Dad shook his head. "I had to keep you and your siblings and your mom safe. Besides, do you think it would help if they knew they were right? There's nothing they can do about it. I never wanted to give them false hope."

Cyra sank into a chair at the tiny table, her cheeks stained red. "I wish you would have told me the truth. I feel like an idiot. I had no idea what the storm was, or that so many people lived outside of it. I thought it was just something we learned to use to protect our City, and that we were so smart for learning how to harness the wind power."

He gave a small smile. "Don't feel dumb. Why would you know any different? You're a kid. You can only know what the adults tell you."

The normal, defiant expression appeared on Cyra's face. "Yeah, well, now I have beef with Mom and Dad. Why didn't they tell me?"

Dad leaned forward. "No, don't blame them. They don't know either. Trust me, I've spent enough time with them to be sure of that. It's also not their fault that they are ingrained with the xenophobia of outsiders, or that their mission in life is to protect the City. The only people to blame are the Renwicks. That family created the storm, and they're responsible for brainwashing everyone here. Very few people know the truth about the storm. Only the people the Renwicks trust to help keep up the storm."

I threw my hands up in exasperation. "Dad, if you know all this, then why are you so happy to stay? It's not right to let them win."

"Ash, you don't understand what you are dealing with." He reached for my hand, his eyes pleading. "The technology behind this storm is so powerful, and it can be unleashed anywhere in the world. Millions of lives could be at risk. Don't you think it's better that it's contained here?"

Tears of frustration filled my eyes. I hated being trapped. "I guess."

Dad rubbed my back. "Listen, just hang in there. You really will enjoy living here. My best advice is to settle in. Play nice, do what you're told, and show Adele you're committed to the City. Now tell me, you were about to graduate high school, right? Are you old enough for that?"

I couldn't help but laugh at the look of disbelief on his face. "Yeah, Dad. I'm eighteen."

He shook his head. "Okay, so what were you planning to do after graduation?"

It was a simple question, but it was like lemon juice pouring on an open wound. My original plan had been to go to Eckman University on the Western Slope with Mason, my unofficial high school boyfriend. He and I liked each other for years, before finally confessing to each other how we felt at the beginning of our senior year. We couldn't officially date, because Mason's mom wouldn't allow dating. But he was my first kiss, and we made plans to go to school together. But then Mason sprung the news that he was accepted to the Air Force Academy, when he never even told me he applied. And then he had the audacity to tell me that he didn't want to have to think about me while he was in the Academy, so we should go our separate ways.

I didn't tell Dad any of that, though. It wasn't worth rehashing.

Cyra wiggled her eyebrows. "Luca, right?"

I made a face. "Uh, I'm not sure what you mean. But I guess none of my plans matter now. I mean, I need some time to figure everything out. I guess I do want to talk to the rest of the Storm Chasers to find out what they're going to do."

She jumped up. "Oh jeez. I forgot. I came here to tell you that Miri is back. Apparently, she's my new roommate."

"Really? Is she okay?"

She gave me a weird look. "Of course she is. I mean, she'll sleep the whole night, because the healing chamber makes you pretty tired. But I was supposed to come and tell you that Mom will serve you all breakfast in the morning, before you have to report to City Hall for your work assignments."

I shook my head. "I really want to see the medical center. I can't believe that they could just heal her like that."

Cyra shrugged and headed for the door. "I guess I'll see you in the morning. You too, Jonah?"

Dad grinned and nodded, and Cyra left, letting the screen door slam behind her.

"I've always liked her," he said. "She reminded me of you. Maybe because she was about the age you were the last time I saw you when I met her."

A wave of fatigue washed over me, and I looked at the bed. "I can't think anymore. I need sleep."

He nodded and studied my face. "Ashlyn, I'm so glad to see you. I can't tell you how happy I am. I never dreamed I would get to see any of my family again, and here you are. Rest, baby girl. We have all the time in the world to catch up. Tomorrow is the first day of a new life."

I nodded and covered a yawn as I headed to the bathroom. I was out of energy to argue. But tomorrow would *not* be the first day of a new life. Tomorrow would be the first day of the countdown to the end of Goliath.

CHAPTER 7

I HAVE ALWAYS BEEN a morning person. Mom said that when I was little, she asked me why I had to get up so early, and she said I'd replied, "Because I'm too excited to start the day!" My siblings were all content to snooze until noon if Mom would let them, but my eyes always seemed to pop open as soon as the sky lightened.

Which is why I was so confused when I woke up in Dad's pool house, and the sun was almost to the middle of the sky. I had never slept so late. A look at the clock told me that it was already early afternoon.

I sat still as I let my eyes roam around the bungalow. Dad wasn't on the couch, and the bathroom door was open, which meant he was gone. I finally saw the piece of paper on the tiny table. It took me a minute to remember that this City did a lot of things from the past, including writing notes on actual paper for each other.

Ash,

You looked so peaceful sleeping that I couldn't bring myself to wake you up. I'm going to work, and will be back by 4:00. You can go to Gwen's for food. She makes a mean breakfast burrito.

Don't worry about Adele's meeting. There is plenty of time for that. Stay close to the bungalow today.

I love you and I'm so glad you're here.
Love, Dad

I sighed. I didn't want to stick close to the bungalow, but I was stuck. I had no idea where to go or what to do next, and I had no idea where any of the rest of the Storm Chasers were.

Then I remembered Miri was staying with Cyra in the main house. I hurried into the bathroom for a quick shower that turned into a long one once I felt how warm the water was. I put my wet, short hair back into two low mini-buns, threw on the last clean shirt I had and the same pair of cargo pants that I had worn for the last week, and hurried up to Cyra's house.

I hesitated for a moment before entering through the back door without knocking. The kitchen was empty, although it still carried the smell of something spicy. I followed the sound of music from a movie to the room at the front of the house.

Miri and Jack sat on a couch, watching a large black rectangle mounted on the wall.

"What is that?" Of all the questions I had, that was the first one that popped out of my mouth.

Jack turned, his eyes bright. "It's called a TV. They are, like, individual units that show videos and stuff. They don't embed screens into walls here."

Miri gave a grin and held up a black stick. "This is a remote. And it's the only thing that controls it."

Her voice brought me back to reality. "Oh my gosh, Miri. How are you?" I rushed to the chair next to the couch and sat.

She shrugged. "I'm fine. Like, completely fine."

"What happened?"

She shook her head. "I don't really know. I remember getting tossed by that dang tornado, and everything hurt so much. I couldn't focus on anything else. I kind of remember Luca being there, but the next thing I remember is waking up in this white box. I thought for sure I had died, and I was in a coffin or something. But then a woman opened a lid and smiled at me, and told me it was time to get out. And I was ready. It was like I had had an amazing nap, and I was energized and ready to go."

My mouth dropped open. "Did they tell you that you were paralyzed?"

"Jack did. But how was that possible? I mean, I'm fine. People don't just take a nap, then wake up ready to go if they're paralyzed."

Jack shrugged and stretched out his arm that was perfectly normal. "People don't put a brace on their broken arm and have it ready to go in an hour either, but here we are. I'm just telling you what I saw. You couldn't move in the Turtle. You didn't even flinch when Ginger poked your leg with a sharp tool."

Miri settled back on the couch and put her feet up on the coffee table. "Well, I'm fine now. Even though Gwen says I have to sit on the couch for the next day or so. But I don't want to. What's the plan?"

I slouched in the comfy chair. "How much do you know about what's happened?"

"You made it to the Eye, Chip told you he got us here, Matteo is a rat sell-out, you found your dad, and now they expect us to become happy City-folk because Goliath is super strong again."

I burst out laughing, even though it wasn't funny. "Yeah, that's exactly what has happened."

She looked proud of herself. "I'm glad you found your dad. But what's next?"

My stomach gave a loud growl. "What's next is I need to eat. I guess I slept for, like, eighteen hours."

Jack nodded and jumped up. "I'll go flash cook you a burrito. I mean, microwave. They don't have flash cookers here. It's like the pioneer days. But Gwen's breakfast burritos are killer. You have to have one."

I grinned as he sprinted into the kitchen. Tears filled my eyes. I was so glad we had found him. All of them.

Miri grunted. "But seriously, are we stuck here?"

I sighed. "It looks that way. Did they tell you that there are tornados guarding the road out of here? Luca and I tried to leave, but we stopped when we saw them. That's when we found you."

"Yeah. But what if they're lying?"

I shook my head. "They're not. Ginger's tech pad said the winds were already over two hundred miles per hour. Which means we have to figure out how to stop the storm ourselves. I mean, the whole thing is being run from this City. There's got to be a way to shut it down."

Miri pushed a button on the remote, and the TV turned black. "If your dad couldn't, how can we?"

I scowled. "Dad never tried. Matteo told him they'd wipe out Denver if he ever tried, so he didn't because he thought he was protecting us. But I guess I'm going to forgive him for that, because he believed it was what he had to do."

Miri leaned forward, a compassionate look replacing her normally cynical look. "After what I've heard, I think Chip would have done it. Wipe out Denver, I mean."

I nodded. "Yeah, I'm sure you're right. Anyway, I think we can shut it down, because we have a team. Dad was by himself."

Miri's eyes twinkled. "Yes. I love it. So, what do we do?"

"I have no idea. I mean, somehow we've got to get into the Weather Production facility. But there's no way they're just going to let us walk in there."

Jack came back with an amazing smelling burrito on a plate next to a dish of salsa. "You'll want to pour a little bit of that salsa on each bite. Trust me."

I did what he asked and groaned in pleasure as the flavors of egg, cheese, and potatoes exploded on my tongue. Jack and Miri laughed, and my cheeks warmed in embarrassment. But that didn't stop me from taking another bite and making yummy sounds again.

Miri leaned back as she watched me eat. "I guess they're going to assign us jobs or something? Gwen said I didn't have to go today, because I needed a full day's rest after being in the chamber. But do you think they'd give us jobs in Weather Production?"

"No way."

We all jumped at Cyra's voice. She stood in the doorway, a scowl on her face. "I snuck into Adele's meeting, even though I wasn't supposed to be there. She assigned Luca and Hugh to maintenance at City Hall, which means they'll be fixing toilets for years. She tried to assign Miri and Ashlyn to housekeeping, meaning you'd be mopping the floors of City Hall every day for the rest of your lives. But

Jonah convinced Adele to let Ashlyn work with him. I guess you can't cause trouble if you have a babysitter."

Miri scowled. "Wait, I still have to mop floors?"

Cyra nodded, but then her face brightened a bit. "Jack gets to work with me in landscaping. We need someone to push wheelbarrows of dirt and stuff."

Jack grinned and flexed his arms. "Perfect."

"Hold on," I said. "I don't even know what Dad does. What will I be doing?"

Cyra gave me an odd look. "He works at the supply warehouse. I don't know what he does either. Whatever it is, I'm sure it's super boring. That building looks like a real snooze-fest, without any windows at all. But all our supplies come out of that building and go to the distribution centers."

Miri looked troubled. "So they're going to keep us away from Weather Production."

Cyra nodded. "Oh yeah. I also forgot to mention that you'll be working twelve-hour shifts. Adele said it's only fair, since you haven't been contributing to our City the way everyone else has. So you need to do some catch up work."

My mouth dropped open. "Can she do that?"

She shrugged. "I'm sure your dad won't make you work that much."

I gave a derisive chuckle. "Well played, I guess. Keep us super busy, so when we aren't working, we'll be too tired to do anything else."

Miri rolled her eyes. "Jokes on her. We're not that soft."

I took a deep breath. "Where is everyone now? Luca, Silas, Ginger. And what about Matteo?"

Cyra rolled her eyes again. "Oh, Matteo is with Adele. Like, he's getting the royal treatment. She 'took custody' of him this morning, but of course that means he gets to stay in the Mayor's Mansion."

I growled. "I'm sure that's Chip's doing. A reward for a stupid job well done."

"Luca and Hugh went right to work. Nash is the head of maintenance, and he was at the meeting, so he took them right away."

My stomach twisted. "Is Nash a good guy?"

Cyra nodded. "Oh yeah. He's, like, practically my grandpa. But he also follows everything Adele says, so if she says to put them to work, then that's what he'll do."

I stopped talking and focused on finishing my burrito. I wanted to figure out how to break into the Weather Production facility, but maybe it would be smart to play along for a little while to get the lay of the land.

I stared at the last bite as my throat closed. I wanted Mom. And Trig. And Dasha. But who knows how long it would be before I got to see them again? I felt a little relief, knowing that Chip was going to tell them I made it here safely, but then anger burned in my belly. I didn't want to feel relief or be thankful to him for anything.

A chime sounded, and Jack, Miri, and I looked around in confusion.

Cyra laughed. "It's a doorbell, you weirdos."

Miri rolled her eyes. "We have door notifications that show up on wall screens, if that's what you're saying. Just not weird bells."

Cyra giggled as she threw open the front door, but her giggle and smile died. She folded her arms and glared out the screen door. "What do you want?"

A male voice answered her, sounding contrite and pleading. "Come on, Cyr. Let me in?"

Cyra shook her head. "No way, you jerk. You almost killed me."

"I didn't mean to! I thought I dropped the funnel far enough away from your signal. There must be something wrong with the sensors."

Cyra heaved out an enormous sigh and pushed open the door. A guy about my age stepped into the house. His hair was combed and was full of some kind of product that made it stay in place. He wore a light blue button-down shirt that was tucked into his khaki pants. He was as preppy as Cyra was not. He stopped short as soon as he saw the rest of us sitting in the room.

I twisted my mouth. "You must be Pax."

He looked at me in surprise. "How did you know that?"

I grinned as Cyra widened her eyes at me, and I ignored her obvious signals to shut up. "Because Cyra said she knew a guy in Weather Production, and only someone in Weather Production, could drop a funnel, right?"

He glanced at Cyra, fear draining the blood from his face. "You told them about Weather Production?"

She rolled her eyes, then left him at the door to flop down on the couch. "I mean, duh. They already kind of knew about it. Besides, they were with me when you almost killed me, so you almost killed them, too."

Sorrow filled Pax's eyes. "I'm so sorry, guys. I really am. It's not supposed to do that. And now Mom is so mad at me that I'm probably going to get demoted to the Wind Data Record team."

Cyra folded her arms. "Yeah, well, maybe that's for the best."

Pax crossed the room and sat next to Cyra. "Please, Cyr. I didn't realize you were so close. I promise."

Miri leaned forward. "I know how you can make it up to us."

Pax turned to her. "Anything. I mean it."

She grinned. "Can you get me a job in Weather Production?"

He looked shocked. "What? No way."

"Come on. Adele already assigned me to housekeeping. Doesn't the Weather Production facility need housekeepers?"

My mouth dropped open at her brilliance. Of course. That would be perfect. A tiny step inside the door, but at least it would be a step.

Pax looked dubious. "Um, I don't know. I mean, you have to have some pretty high clearance to work in that building. There's no way you could get that."

Cyra put her hand on Pax's arm. "Oh, come on. Security is tight in every section. It's not like she could get into any classified rooms. She'd just be emptying trash cans out of the outer offices and cleaning the bathrooms and kitchen and stuff."

Pax's cheeks stained pink as he looked at Cyra's hand on his arm. "I guess you're right. But how am I supposed to do that? Mom already assigned her to City Hall."

Cyra scooted closer. "Just tell Raina that Adele said she could switch. Raina never questions you."

Miri leaned forward. "Who's Raina?"

A wicked grin stretched across Cyra's face. "She runs the housekeeping department at City Hall, and she *loooooves* Pax."

Pax's blush deepened. "Uh, nothing is going on between me and Raina."

Cyra grinned. "Duh, dummy. But Raina hopes that something will happen, so she does whatever you say, right? She's tight with Dez at Weather Production. Dez literally doesn't care about this stuff and will be happy to finally have someone to help her. You can tell Raina that Miri will still fill out the City Hall time card."

I cleared my throat. "Won't Adele realize Miri isn't at City Hall every day?"

Pax shook his head. "Mom is too busy. She never asks about housekeeping. She trusts Raina to take care of all of that. Besides, I'll tell Raina that if Mom ever asks, she should just tell her that Miri is in a different part of the building."

I folded my arms and grinned. "Then it's settled. Get Miri a job at housekeeping at Weather Production, and all is forgiven."

Pax looked around the room. "Well, okay, I guess." He shifted on his feet, then leaned in closer to Cyra. "Can we talk, like, outside or something?"

Cyra sniffed. "Why? We don't have to keep secrets from these guys. They're legit."

Pax's cheeks turned pink. "Um, because I came here to ask if you wanted to go to the party with me."

Jack leaned forward. "Party? What party?"

Cyra rolled her eyes. "Oh yeah. Adele told everyone at the meeting that there's a party at City Hall and City Park tonight. It's to celebrate some dumb Weather Production thing. They do that a lot."

Pax's eyes flashed. "It's not dumb. We got Goliath to surpass the upper limits of Category Five, like, two days ago. We've been able to sustain a Category Six for over twenty-four hours. It's one of the most important achievements Weather Production has ever done."

Miri's expression darkened. "You mean, *other* than capturing a hurricane and keeping it going for fifty years?"

Pax grinned. "Well, yeah. It's amazing, right?"

Cyra groaned. "Who cares? The parties are lame. I don't want to go."

I made eye contact with Miri, and I could tell she was thinking the same thing. The rest of the team might be there. We needed to be at that party. "I do."

Miri nodded. "Me too. We'll go with you, Pax."

Pax looked lost. That was clearly not what he was thinking.

Cyra groaned. "Ugh, fine. I'll go if you all go."

My heart lifted. This was going to work.

CHAPTER 8

THE PEOPLE OF THE City worked quickly. Or maybe I had slept longer and harder than I thought. Whatever it was, a massive fair had appeared right outside of City Hall and throughout City Park.

"Where do they store these rides?" Miri asked, gaping at the gigantic Ferris wheel that sat in front of City Hall.

I shrugged and eyed the tilt-a-whirl. "Probably at Dad's warehouse. I don't know. I'll tell you when I start there tomorrow."

Cyra snorted. "These are baby rides. The same ones they pull out for everything."

Jack bounced up and down like a little kid in a candy store. "I've always wanted to try rides! Why did they get outlawed back home? They look awesome."

"Because they were dangerous. People fell out of them and died and stuff," Miri said.

I grinned. "But here they can just pop you in a box and heal you instantly. I get it. Don't you want to try one?"

She shuddered. "Getting tossed by a tornado was as close to a carnival ride as I want to be on. I'm good, thanks."

As much as I wanted to try a ride, I wanted to find the team more. Okay, fine, I wanted to find Luca more. I hadn't seen him in over twenty-four hours.

I was amazed at how many people milled around. I had almost forgotten there were so many people who lived here. It turned out Luca, Silas, Ginger and Hugh were easy to find, because the people of the City were giving them a wide berth. The entire park was pretty crowded, but there was almost a line formed going around the spot in the courtyard that we had sat in the day we got there.

Luca's eyes lit up when he saw me, and warmth curled in my belly at the sight of his grin. Miri, Jack, Cyra, and I made our way over to them.

Miri looked around. "What's going on? Does it smell bad over here or something?"

Silas grinned. "Everyone must think we're infected with hurricane germs or something. No one wants to come within ten feet of us."

I sank down on a bench. "Good. I'm not in the mood to socialize with the locals. Where have you all been?"

Luca sat next to me, much closer than he needed to. I tried to scoot closer without being obvious. "They put me, Jack and Hugh up in this spare room in the maintenance shed."

I wrinkled my nose. "Is it nice?"

Hugh stretched his legs out. "It looks likes the shelter where we found Cyra."

Jack nodded. "There's one bed right now, but Nash said that he could get us bunk beds."

Silas put his arm around Ginger. I tried to not react, but this still wasn't something I was used to. "Ging is across the street from me. So that works out." They locked gazes in a way that made me blush.

A loud cheer erupted from the crowd, and we turned to see Adele and three men file out of City Hall onto the front steps, where someone had set up a box and a stick. Adele waved at the crowd, singling out a few people here and there and mouthing words to them.

She stepped up to the box and leaned in toward the stick. "Hello, my beautiful City!" Her voice echoed across the park.

"Whoa," Jack said. "It's an old-school voice amplifier."

Cyra gave him an odd glance. "You mean the mic?"

Pax snorted and folded his arms. "Where did you guys say you were from?"

I narrowed my eyes. "From a place that doesn't use old technology."

Adele waited for the cheers to die down, a gracious, nauseating smile on her face. "We're here to celebrate another amazing achievement by our fantastic Weather Production team. For the first time in the history of the natural world, we have witnessed and recorded a hurricane that surpasses the top of the Saffir-Simpson Hurricane Wind Scale. Not only have we recorded it, but we have sustained it. For the past twenty-nine hours, Goliath has held steady at two hundred and four miles per hour!"

The crowd exploded with excitement as confetti cannons erupted from the sides of City Hall. An honest-to-goodness band with a tuba and everything burst into a driving march. There was so much hugging, crying, and high-fiving that you would have thought their team won the gold medal at the Olympics.

I shook my head. "This is crazy."

"Actually, it's pretty impressive," Ginger said. "Man, I wish I could see how they did it."

Miri scoffed. "But they won't let us anywhere near Weather Production."

She sighed. "Yeah. I got assigned to work in the library. It's cool in there with all the books, but I hoped I'd get to learn more about their tech. I wanted to adapt what we brought."

That reminded me. "What *did* we bring? I never asked you what you stopped for in Dallas."

Her eyes took on a wicked gleam. "Four EMPs and two signal jammers. But now that I've seen the storm and those pillars, I'm not sure it's enough. What I really need is access to their mainframe. There has to be a master control we can infect with spyware and shut down."

The crowd quieted down and Adele leaned down to speak. "That's right. It is definitely something to celebrate. Our Weather Production team is filled with absolute geniuses who can bend nature to their will. But we also have to remember our patron outside the storm, who has given us everything we need to make this happen. Therefore, I decree that every year this day will be known as Sinclair Scale Day, and it will always be a City-wide holiday!"

Again, the crowd broke out into thunderous applause as my stomach turned at the mention of Chip and his contribution to this nightmare. The cheers lasted way too long.

Adele let the cheers die down, then continued. "Today, I also want to celebrate someone in particular. I'm sure you all are aware that we have some guests who came in through the storm just to live with us. What you might not know is they were escorted in by one of our good friends outside the storm, who has been helping us sustain not only Goliath but our lifestyle in our great City. Let's give a warm welcome to Matteo Chapman!"

The crowd erupted in cheers again as Matteo stepped up to the mic. "Uh, hello, City!" He sounded hesitant, yet raised his voice at the end in a way that said he expected everyone to cheer. The crowd clapped politely. "Thanks for having me. And my brother, and my friends. I hope you'll get to know us soon, and we look forward to getting to know you."

I turned to Silas. "What is he doing?"

He shrugged, his eyes narrowed.

Matteo went on. "Uh, that's my brother back there, and everyone else. Um, you all know Jonah Booker. Well, that's his daughter, Ashlyn. The one next to Cyra. Wave, Ashlyn!" I gave him a dirty look and shook my head as hundreds of heads swivelled toward us. Except these eyes were all filled with distrust. I felt like an animal in a zoo. I squirmed a little and stepped behind Luca. Luca folded his arms and gave a chin-up nod to the crowd.

"Anyway, you should stop by and introduce yourselves. And, uh, thanks again for having us." Matteo backed away and looked to Adele for rescue.

Adele returned to the mic. "This new group will be a welcome addition to our City. So let the party begin! Enjoy yourselves everyone! Oh, and be sure to check out the pie stand. Greta just harvested the first crop of blackberries of the season, and you'll want to be the first to have a piece of her pie!"

The band kicked back up and everyone broke away to enjoy the carnival. Our group stayed where we were.

"I'm not so sure they want us at their party," Hugh said, a slight grin on his face.

"What was that about?" Miri asked Silas. "Why did Matteo call us out like that?"

He sighed and shrugged. "Probably to make things better, by getting people to like us."

"Hello, friends!" Adele's musical voice broke into our group. We reluctantly opened up the circle to let her and Matteo in. "I'm so glad you could join us for this special day."

We were silent. I got the feeling she was expecting us to say thank you or something, but we all just looked at her.

"Well, I hope you're all settling in okay," she said, after a tense few seconds. "I'm glad you were here for this celebration. It's important for you all to see what community is about."

I channelled my inner Cyra and rolled my eyes. "We know what community is, Adele. We all come from communities."

She pressed her lips into a tight smile. "Well, I'm sure they're not as tight-knit as ours. But now you're a part of this family, and it was important that you meet everyone, don't you think?"

I was about to tell Adele what I thought about meeting everyone when I caught Silas' eye. He gave a slight shake of his head, and I stood down.

"I'll admit this is not how we were hoping for things to go, but we're grateful for your hospitality," Ginger said.

Adele smiled at her, and for a moment, it almost looked like a genuine smile. "Well, I appreciate honesty. And your gratitude. If you just give us a chance, you'll see that we're all going to do great things together."

I couldn't hold it in any longer. "Great things? Like, working twelve-hour shifts like slaves for you people? Aren't there labor laws?"

Her eyes narrowed as she pierced me with her gaze. "It's not for long. Just to catch you up to how we do things around here. I promise that this kind of immersion will be better for everyone in the long run." She seemed to remember who she was and pasted the smile back on her face. "I will work diligently with City Hall to set up a fair immigration process, and we'll be able to give you full citizen status in no time. You'll have to bear with us; we've never had to integrate outsiders before."

I swallowed back a gag and prayed that she would go away soon. "You mean, besides Dad, right?"

A stricken look filled her eyes, but she recovered quickly. "Yes, besides Jonah. I meant an entire group." She turned to Pax, a slight frown on her face. "Where have you been? I asked you to be home two hours ago so you could join us on stage."

Pax dipped his head. "Yeah, uh, sorry. I wanted to see Cyra."

Adele's icy gaze settled on Cyra. "Oh, that's right. You hadn't seen her since her little adventure. Well, fine, I guess. But you need to go join your great-grandfather right now. We have ceremonial pictures to take for the newsletter."

Pax's cheeks turned red and anger flashed in his eyes as he spun around and headed for City Hall. My heart went out to him. He was way too old to be treated like a naughty boy by his mommy.

Adele turned back to us, her phony smile back in place. "Well, enjoy! Try the pies." She sailed away, waving at the people who dared venture close to us outsiders.

I couldn't say which was worse: Fake Diplomatic Adele, or Strict Parent Adele.

Matteo watched her go, fear in his eyes. I didn't think he expected to be left behind. He turned back to us, but no one said anything.

"Uh, so, how do you like your new jobs?" he asked.

My jaw dropped. "Seriously?"

Miri snorted. "What's *your* job, Matteo? Or do you get to just lay by Adele's pool for the rest of your life?"

Matteo's face flushed. "I'm not freeloading, if that's what you're asking. I have work to do at City Hall." He glanced at Silas. "I'm not a bum. I work hard."

Silas clenched his jaw. "Can it, Matteo. We're not ready for small talk with you. So congratulations on getting a job. I'm sure I'll see you around."

Matteo's face fell at his brother's dismissal. Then his expression hardened. "Got it. Loud and clear, brother. Bye." He turned and marched away.

Silas' face twitched, and Ginger grabbed his hand, compassion filling her eyes.

"Enough of that. What's the next step?" Silas asked.

Miri folded her arms. "Well, Pax is going to get me a job in housekeeping at Weather Production. So I guess I'll try to learn what I can there."

Ginger sighed. "I think that's all we can do for now. Do our jobs, learn what we can. Then meet up once a week and share intel, like we did with the Storm Chasers."

Silas cocked his eyebrow. "We're the Storm Breakers now."

She rolled her eyes. "Whatever."

I gazed at the party going on all around us. "Yeah, I guess that's all we can do. But I hate it."

Ginger reached out and squeezed my arm. "You haven't been with us long, Ashlyn, but trust us. Our patience will serve us well. We'll find the crack."

Luca put his arm around me. "Yeah, Dad would have agreed. So I'm going to fix toilets, but you better believe I will be looking in every single door I can."

"And I'm on board, guys," Cyra said. "I'll wear down Pax. I bet he'll tell me how we can shut off the storm."

Ginger eyed her. "Okay, but be subtle. I'm serious. You can't just demand answers, or they'll come after us. Do they have jail here?"

Cyra looked subdued for the first time since I had met her. "I understand. I promise I'll be cool. I, uh, I don't know anything about jail. But I don't want any of you to get in trouble."

Luca let go of me and started walking backward. "Well, come on. Let's at least see if we can have some pie."

We all agreed and moved as a group toward the fair. If we couldn't shut down Goliath tonight, then we might as well have pie.

CHAPTER 9

I STIRRED MY SOUP and scowled. I never imagined that the main diet of the people in the City would be plant-based. They had chickens, but they mostly used them for egg production. Dad explained with their limited resources, the City just couldn't support much meat production. They had meat, but by now, everyone was used to the vegetarian lifestyle, so they didn't like it.

My throat closed, and I pushed the bowl away. Two weeks had passed, and the Storm Chasers had made zero progress on our objective. I mean, the Storm Breakers. I couldn't get used to that name.

The Storm Breakers hadn't been able to meet. I had hardly seen Luca and Silas. Adele's plan was working. They kept us so busy that all we could do was go home and sleep when we weren't at work. We hadn't been able to meet up even once.

The only reason I ever saw Miri was because she was still in Cyra's house. And the only reason I ever saw Jack was because he worked with Cyra, and she brought him home for dinner. Most nights, Dad and I ate with Gwen, Xander, and the crew that lived in their house. Miri, Jack, Cyra, and I would hang out in the backyard as soon as the dishes were done each night, but we never had much to say. Our jobs were boring. Miri was emptying trash and cleaning toilets all day. Jack was pushing wheelbarrows, so he always fell asleep on the lounge chairs.

My job was the most boring of all. Dad ran the warehouse that held supplies for distribution, and all he would let me do was sit in his windowless office and update the spreadsheets with the numbers of supplies that were distributed the day before. You would think that a city that could instantly heal someone of a spinal injury would also have the ability to link up a tech pad to instantly record what supplies were going out in real time. He tried to explain that the City committed their technology to other things, like Weather Production and medical advances, and that most other places had to do it the old-fashioned way. But that was lame. And lazy.

My theory? Adele wanted to keep the entire population of the City too tired to ask questions by making them do everything the hard way. Everyone around here worked long, hard hours, then fell into bed at nine o'clock every night, dead to the world.

Dad pushed the plate of sourdough bread toward me. "Here. Gwen made this today, and it's still warm. Have you tried her strawberry jam yet?"

I wrinkled my nose and wished we were eating in the big house with the rest of the group today. Miri and Jack would have had something to say about the jam. "Reuben lured us with strawberry jam in Goliath. Then he tried to hold us captive in Ousley and steal our med supplies."

Dad raised his eyebrows. "You went to Ousley? I remember them. They were nice people. I can't believe Deacon would keep you there. Who is Reuben?"

"Reuben was Matteo's buddy. Which, of course, looking back, means we should have not trusted Matteo anymore. Deacon didn't keep us. It was Reuben and Murphy, the mayor."

Dad chuckled as he slurped up some more soup. "Ah, yes. Murphy. He was kind of an idiot."

I sighed and reached for the jam. Anything to help add variety to the veggie noodle soup. A wave of exhaustion washed over me as I lifted my arm, and my eyes filled with tears. I shouldn't be this tired. I wasn't doing a physical job like everyone else, but sitting in that dark room in front of a screen all day was so draining.

"Ash? What's wrong?"

I wiped my nose. "Nothing."

"Come on. Talk to me. Maybe I can help."

I looked at him, and the compassionate, hopeful look on his face made me angry. "Oh really? Can you help me get home by Saturday so I can walk at graduation?"

His face fell. "Oh, Ash. I'm so sorry. I forgot all about that."

I grabbed a piece of bread and tore it into tiny pieces, channeling my rage into something meaningless. "Just like you forgot about us this whole time."

Dad looked up at me, frustration filling his face for the first time since I got here. "I'm tired of this. You cannot throw this in my face every single time you're upset. I did what I did to protect you, and I'm not sorry for that. You all got to live. It was worth every sacrifice I made. I'm going to say this one last time, and then trust that you are mature enough to remember it. I did not forget you. I've thought about you all every single day for the last ten years, praying that your lives were happy, healthy, and whole. I'm so sorry that you all had to walk through the grief of my disappearance, but I'd rather have you all grieve than die."

My heart pounded as I stared at him. I wanted to fight back. I wanted to scream that he was lying or stupid or that if he had been a real man, he would have found a way.

Then a sob erupted out of my chest, and I buried my head in my arms. I also had kept secrets to keep people safe. Maybe if I had told Mom everything from the beginning, I wouldn't be here. I should have told her what I heard Chip say outside of her office, and I should have told her how Chip threatened our whole family that day on our driveway. Maybe she could have stopped the hurricane from USHA headquarters, or at least exposed Chip for what he was and taken away his power.

But I wanted to protect her, so I ran away into the storm. Just like Dad. And now we were both trapped.

Dad got up and dragged his chair around the table to sit next to me. "Ashlyn, I'm so sorry you're missing your graduation. What can I do to make it up to you? Do you want to have a party or something? We can invite all of your friends. I know you haven't seen that boy in a while."

I chuckled despite myself. "That boy? You mean Luca?"

He shrugged. "I'm not good with names."

I bumped him with my shoulder and grabbed the jam. "What about Disney World? Isn't that around here? I mean, is it in the Eye?"

He grinned. "No, sorry. The old site is right in the eyewall, so it got blown away after Goliath settled over the city."

I wasn't hungry anymore, so I pushed my bowl aside. I reached for the iron pills that Dad had given me since the first night I arrived. Everyone in the City took them to help supplement what they weren't getting from their plant-based diet. I was so exhausted at the end of each day that I slept like the dead and thought my iron was still too low. "Why do they call it the City? Isn't this Orlando?"

Dad stood and gathered the dishes to be washed. "I'm sure you've realized now that these people have rejected pretty much everything about the United States. I've been told that as soon as people realized the storm was here to stay, and that they were protected in the Eye, they decided to stop calling this area by the old name."

I raised an eyebrow. "They decided? Or Ashton Renwick did?"

He shrugged. "If you ask anyone, they'll tell you that all the original survivors decided together. But the Renwick family are experts at making people think something is their idea. They are the ultimate puppet-masters."

That surprised me. I always thought Chip was the ultimate puppet-master. It made me wonder if he really was the hurricane keeper, after all.

"So, they didn't convince everyone to rename the city to Renwickville?"

"No, because the Renwick family is more subtle than that."

I let out a laugh, then sighed as I moved to the oversized chair next to the couch that had become Dad's bed. "So, no Disney World."

Dad wiped his hands on a towel, then sat on the couch. "No. But what about the party?"

I rolled my eyes. "Oh yeah. We can have tofu dogs."

"Come on. What can we do to celebrate your graduation? You may not have finished the last couple of weeks, but that was unforeseen. So you still deserve some kind of celebration because you completed high school." Dad's voice became choked. "And I missed all of the celebrations for your siblings, so please let me be a part of this one."

I leaned back and stared at the ceiling fan. An idea popped into my head and I sat up. "I don't want a party. That would be too weird. But I've got an idea for a present."

Dad smiled. "What? Anything."

"A tour."

His grin melted into confusion. "A tour of what?"

"This whole city. All the way around. I want to see everything. I want to see the Weather Production facility, and the Medical facility. I want to see what it's like on the other side of the city. I've been stuck here ever since we got here. I've seen Cyra's street, the supply warehouse, and City Hall. That's it."

Dad looked nervous. "I'm not sure it's a good idea, Ash."

"Why not? I'm pretty sure you said that we would when I first got here. What changed?"

"Adele doesn't like people poking around."

I tucked my feet up under me, confident that I had a good plan. "I'm not asking to go *in* Weather Production. I just want to see where it is. I mean, are people allowed to travel around the city?"

"Of course they are." Dad leaned back, worry written all over his face. "But I guess no one really does. They just stick to their area and their job."

I felt triumphant. "See? So how do you know Adele wouldn't like it?"

He twisted his mouth. "Well, I can tell you that she is doing everything she can to keep you on a short leash. I had to swear on my life you'd stay with me in the warehouse, and she reminded me it took seven years to build my reputation here, but that could be shattered in minutes."

My heart sped up, but I tried to keep my face calm. I didn't want to jeopardize anything for Dad. But I had to get more information about this whole city if I was going to come up with any ideas on how to shut down the storm and get back home. "Come on, Dad. Tell her it's my graduation present. And can I bring a friend?"

His eyes narrowed. "Which friend?"

My cheeks grew warm, but I kept my chin up. "Luca, of course."

He scowled. "What, not Miri?"

"Dad."

He sighed. "Okay. I'll ask."

I squealed, jumped up, and threw my arms around his neck. "Yay! Thank you, Daddy."

He wrapped me in a hug and kissed the side of my head. "All I can do is ask. If she says no, we'll have to come up with something else."

I sobered up and sat back down. "Have you ever been around the city?"

A sly grin appeared on Dad's face. "Yeah. I was the first outsider ever to come here, so they didn't know what to do with me for a couple of weeks. So I would explore. They are very confident that no one can leave, so no one asked questions. I finally asked for a job once I had been around the entire eye."

I rolled my eyes. "So you realize that the only reason they are treating me and my friends like prisoners is because Chip told them to."

A look of doubt filled his eyes. "I guess so. Honey, I'm still having a hard time wrapping my mind around the idea that he's in charge of this. Are you sure it isn't Matteo?"

I threw my hands in the air. "Why would Matteo get into the eye, and then order Goliath to be increased so he couldn't get back out?"

Dad took a deep breath in through his nose and slowly let out the air. "I don't know. But what I do know is that the Renwick family is very protective of the storm. The storm has allowed all the advances you see, because it allowed experimentation without oversight and regulation from the government."

This was news. "Experimentation? What do you mean?"

He shrugged. "How else do you invent new technologies? Experimentation. So I know you've got your thing against Chip. I'm saying that it's possible he's just doing what he's told by someone else."

I set my mouth. What was it going to take for him to believe me? And was he right? I was starting to wonder if there would ever be a day when all of my questions would be answered. It seemed like every time I got an answer to a question, a new one popped up.

"I guess it doesn't matter. But I want the full tour of the city."

He nodded, then turned and stretched out on his couch, yawning. "I'll ask in the morning, okay? You've been working so hard that I bet Adele will let us take a few days to go around the entire city. I've got some friends we can stay with on the east side."

He had barely finished talking when he let out a snore. I frowned. I had learned two things about Dad in these last couple of weeks. First was that he had the annoying ability to fall asleep immediately. Second was that he snored like a lumberjack. I had made it my goal to fall asleep before him every night so his snoring wouldn't keep me up.

I sighed and moved to the bathroom to get ready for bed. I'd poke him awake before I settled, and that would give me a few minutes to fall asleep first.

As I brushed my teeth, I realized I asked for the wrong thing for my graduation present. I should have asked for my own housing.

CHAPTER 10

"Seriously?"

"What? It's the same one you've ridden in every day."

I clutched my backpack and stared at the golf cart. "I mean, yeah, but I thought that's just what you used to get to work and back. It's your only vehicle?"

Dad shrugged. "Everyone has them. They're electric, so they can be charged at any building, since they're all equipped with solar panels. As far as I can tell, they haven't used anything bigger than this since the storm settled."

Luca grunted beside me. "But these only go, like, twelve miles per hour."

Dad scowled. "So? You feel the need for speed, son?"

I rolled my eyes. "So that means it'll take a couple of hours to get to the other side of the city. It's not efficient."

He climbed behind the steering wheel. "You can sit up front. Luca can sit in the back."

I gave Luca an apologetic look, and he winked at me before settling into the seat behind Dad. My innards warmed. If Dad was going to be rude to Luca, then I'd sit in the back with him, and Dad could drive us around like a chauffeur.

Dad pulled away from Cyra's house and we hummed down the street. "No one travels far. Families all live within a block or two of each other. And most people live within a few miles of their jobs and City Hall, so it doesn't matter. Only the farmers and the energy harvesters live on the outskirts of town."

So that was the second part of the Renwick plan for societal subjugation. Give people the illusion of being allowed to move freely, but keep them close by giving them lame means of travel. Brilliant.

Dad cleared his throat. "Um, we have to stop at City Hall first."

"Why?"

He gave me a sideways glance. "Adele wanted to chat with you before we left."

My stomach clenched. I had avoided her since the first day we got here. I had nothing to say to her. "About what?"

He shrugged. "It was her condition when I asked about going on the tour."

Did Dad ask how high every time Adele said jump? Why didn't he show some backbone?

Luca put his hand on my shoulder. "Do you want me to go with you?"

Dad tightened his grip on the wheel. "She asked to speak to her alone. Ashlyn, she's harmless. She won't hurt you. You'll have a much better life here if you can get on her good side. I promise. She really doesn't ask for much."

I tried to give Luca a brave smile. "No, I've got it. It's fine. Let's get this over with."

Dad parked in front of City Hall. "Check in at the front desk. You have an appointment."

I marched into the bustling lobby and froze. Everyone stopped and stared at me. It took me a minute to remember that they weren't used to seeing outsiders. I gave an awkward wave, and they slowly went back to their business.

A plump lady with curly hair sat at the giant desk in the middle of the lobby. "Hello! You must be Ashlyn."

I nodded, weirded out that she already knew my name. "Yes. And who are you?"

She giggled. "I'm Portia. I'm just tickled to meet you. What's it like out there?"

I glanced over my shoulder, and she laughed harder.

"No, silly, not outside in the courtyard. I mean *out there*."

"Out in the storm? Or out in the real world?"

Her eyes sparkled. "Any of it. Hey, you want to get coffee sometime? I know it's a lot to ask to give me some of your time on your only day off, but I'd love to talk with you."

"Portia." Adele's sing-songy voice rang out. The hum of the crowd dimmed as everyone smiled at Adele as she glided across the lobby. It gave me the icks, both the way she walked and the way everyone responded to her.

Portia's cheeks stained pink. "Oh, hi, Adele. Your appointment is here."

Adele gave Portia a charming smile. "I see that. Thank you for being so welcoming. That's the reason I gave you this job. That, and the fact that you understand things like discretion and duty."

Portia nodded, her curls bouncing. "For sure. You know I love it here."

"Good. Then remember your real work, okay? Ashlyn, thank you for coming in. Right this way."

I had to force my face to stay neutral as I followed her out of the lobby. I wasn't sure what kind of mob would happen if I rolled my eyes in the presence of all of her sycophants.

She led me down the same hall that we had taken the first day I came. I had been so excited, thinking she was taking me to see Dad. But instead, I was tricked into a horrible video chat with Chip.

I froze when she stopped at the door of the room with the screen. "No."

Adele turned. "Calm down, Sweetie. Chip isn't calling right now."

I narrowed my eyes. "Then what are we doing here?"

She reached out as if she were going to touch my shoulder, but then seemed to think better of it and clasped her hands in front of her. Smart move. "I'm sure this has been difficult for you. It's not easy to settle into a life you didn't plan. But I'm not a monster. My job is to make sure all our citizens are happy and healthy. So when your dad told me what he wanted to do for you as a graduation present, I tried to think of a gift I could give. To show you I'm on your side and want to celebrate this milestone with you."

She looked so proud of herself. Was she expecting a hug or something?

I folded my arms. "Really?"

She nodded. "So I talked to Chip and arranged a special call for you. It's not something we do very often, but this is a very special occasion, isn't it?"

My heart rate picked up as I reached for the door. "Is it my mom?"

She giggled. "Go in and sit down. Press the enter key on the keyboard."

I pushed open the door and slammed it shut, not wanting to risk that she would follow me in to listen in on our conversation. I flew into the seat and pressed the key.

A small buffering circle appeared and seemed to cycle forever. I thought I would crawl out of my skin until the screen changed, and an empty chair appeared on screen.

My heart stopped for a moment before someone sat down.

Mason.

My mouth fell open and my heart sank. I had no words.

"Hey, Ash," he said. He had relief written all over his face. I stood up and turned to leave. I didn't want to talk to him.

"No, wait. I've been so worried about you. Please, stay."

I closed my eyes. Of course, Chip would tell Adele that *this* is who I would want to talk to. He was always creepily invested in my relationship with Mason. He caught us kissing a couple of times, and now I wondered how long he watched us before making his presence known.

And then there was the fact that Chip was the one who helped Mason get into the Air Force Academy. Without Chip's connections to the United States House of Representatives, Mason would have never gotten the recommendation letter he needed to get in.

My throat closed, and I gripped the back of the chair. I would never let Adele bring me in here again.

"Ash, please. I've been so worried. We all have been. I mean, Dasha told us you decided to not go on the senior trip because I went, and I felt terrible. But when we all got home and realized you were missing, you can't imagine the media coverage and the prayer vigils that have gone on around here. Then Chip told your mom that you had made it to the Eye, and everyone was so relieved, but it still really sucked that no one could talk to you. Then Chip called me yesterday and said he arranged a chat with you today, and I can't tell you how happy I was."

Rage filled my chest. I turned and glared at the screen. "Did he tell you I haven't even been able to talk to Mom?"

He frowned. "Really? No, he didn't. He said that the connection to the Eye is really fickle, and that talking to you would be my graduation present."

I threw my hands in the air and sat down. "Mason, Chip is a bad guy. I tried to tell you that. Did you know he basically lured me here? Oh, and that my dad is alive?" I shouted those last words.

He looked stunned. "You always said he was."

I folded my arms. "Yeah. And Chip said he 'paved the way' for me to get here, then cranked up the storm so I couldn't leave, so he could get me out of the way. Just like he did to Dad ten years ago."

Mason sighed. "Chip isn't the bad guy, okay? He told me that USHA has been working with the Air Force and the Space Force to find a way into the Eye, by going up and over it. I'm going to take the Space Force track in the Academy, so I can be a part of that. If we can get in, we can get you out. And Chip is helping with that."

I was speechless. The lengths Chip would go to lie shocked me every time. I don't know why.

I leaned forward. "Listen, I want to talk to my mom. I *need* to talk to her. Can you tell her I'm okay? And that Dad is alive? Please. If she knew that, then at least she'd break off her stupid relationship with him. If I have to be stuck here for the rest of my life, then I can accept it if I knew that at least she broke up with him."

Mason pressed his lips together and rubbed the back of his neck. "Ah, no. I'm sorry. Chip made me sign an NDA. I'm not allowed to talk to anyone about this, not even my mom."

I laughed. I couldn't help it. Of course, he would think that telling *his* mom about this was more important than telling *my* mom.

He scowled. "Come on, Ash. Please. He said if I violate the NDA, I can never talk to you again. And he said he'd tell the U.S. Rep about my lack of trustworthiness, and that she might revoke my admission to the Academy."

I slammed my fist on the desk. "Are you kidding me? This proves Chip's a rat. Can't you see that?"

Mason's eyes filled with pity. *Pity.* "He's just trying to make sure I know how important discretion is."

There was that word again. Discretion. Adele used it with Portia. Now Chip is using it with Mason. It was a manipulative word, designed to prey on someone's sense of character in order to force them to do something.

I rubbed my eyes. "Fine. Whatever. Nice to talk to you, Mason. Goodbye."

"Wait, Ash, I—"

I hit the enter key again to end the call and stared in relief at the black screen.

The door opened and Adele poked her head in.

"All done?"

I spun in the chair and glared at her. "That was the worst graduation present ever."

She looked confused. "What? A call with your boyfriend?"

I rolled my eyes. "He's not my boyfriend. Did Chip tell you that? We broke up. I wanted to talk to my mom."

Uncertainty flashed across her face before she schooled her features. "Oh Sweetie. That's not possible. But you can talk to Mason anytime you want, okay? Chip promised that. I didn't know he wasn't your boyfriend, but he might give you news about your family, right? Put your mind at ease?"

I just wanted to leave. I moved out into the hall and past Adele before stopping.

"What is it that Chip has over you, that you do whatever he asks?"

Adele's eyes flashed, and for the first time, her mask of sunshine slipped. "What makes you think he has anything over me?"

I shrugged. "You're an excellent lap dog, doing whatever he asks. I mean, you're here, thousands of miles away, protected by the storm. And you still seem to let him call all the shots."

Adele took a step toward me and lowered her voice. "Listen, Sweetie. You can believe whatever you want. I really don't care. Just know that the minute you cause trouble or slack off on contributing to our City, I can make life very difficult for you. Or your dad. Or any of your little friends." Her face brightened, and she became Sunshine Queen all over again. "But you're going to have a great life here. So enjoy your tour. You probably won't be able to get out like this again. There's too much work to do. Oh, and tell your dad that I'll chat with him when he gets back about the fact that the output requirements for the warehouse have been increased, so people are going to need to pull double shifts for the foreseeable future."

Adele stepped back and gestured toward the door leading to the lobby, inviting me to leave. I clenched my fists and made myself calmly walk out through the lobby into the courtyard.

"Whoa." Luca's eyes were wide. "What happened?"

Trig had always told me I wore my emotions on my face, no matter what. Apparently, that was still true. I slumped onto the seat of the golf cart. "I don't want to talk about it. Can we go?"

"Oh, Jonah!" Adele's sing-song voice rang out across the courtyard, and I wanted to throw up.

Dad pasted on a pleasant expression as she approached. "Hey, Adele. Thanks so much for letting us go on this tour."

She smiled a sparkling smile, and a wave of nausea swept through me. How could she look so calm and delighted when she had just threatened everyone I knew? She was a sociopath. Just like Chip.

"My pleasure! Celebrations of milestones are important. I have one more present." She handed Dad an envelope. "Here is a key card that will give you access to all the Mayor Cottages around the City. You can stay there. They each have a chef, a groundskeeper, and a housekeeper, so you wouldn't have to worry about anything."

Dad's eyes widened. "Oh, wow. Thank you so much. You didn't have to do that. I planned to stay with Greta and Yuri on the east side."

Adele let out a merry laugh and waved her hand. "Well, when you get to the east side, you can invite them to come stay with you."

"Gosh, thanks again. I don't know what else to say."

"Don't mention it. Just be sure to follow all the directions on that paper. Every single one. I'll see you in two days, though. Remember?"

Dad nodded, and Adele backed away, but not before making eye contact with me. I stared her down until she looked away.

One thought made me smile: soon Adele was going to realize that her first mistake was letting me go on this tour.

CHAPTER 11

The ride away from City Hall stayed silent for about ten minutes. Finally, Dad cleared his throat.

"Ah, I have a confession. I never knew how to handle girl stuff."

I gave him a side glance. "Girl stuff?"

Dad shrugged. "When you girls were upset. Do you want me to ask about it? Or not? Your mom always handled these things."

I sighed and glanced back at Luca. "Adele set up a video chat. With Mason. Like it was part of her dumb graduation present. Oh, and it was Chip's idea."

Luca's mouth dropped open. "Mason?"

"Who's Mason?" Dad asked.

I shifted in the seat. "He was kind of my boyfriend. But not really, because his mom wouldn't allow us to date. We were going to go to Eckman University together, but Mason secretly applied to the Air Force Academy instead, and he got in. Then he decided he didn't want to have to think about me anymore, so we shouldn't be, well, close."

It was still a little painful to say out loud, but I realized it didn't hurt as much as it had a week ago. That seemed like a totally different life.

"What did Mason say?" Luca asked.

I rolled my eyes. "Nothing. Just that Chip told him it was *his* graduation present, to talk to me. And that he had to sign an NDA, so he wasn't allowed to tell Mom or anyone what we talked about, or that we even talked at all."

I couldn't decide whether to tell them anything else. Part of me wanted to. I was so done with keeping secrets because of threats. That's the whole reason Dad and I were stuck in this tropical prison to begin with. But I couldn't help it. I had to do what it took to protect my family and friends, right?

Dad stayed silent while he drove along. He kept his eyes forward and didn't even wave back to the people in passing golf carts who waved at him.

Luca stuck his arm over the seat and grabbed my hand. "Are you okay?"

I squeezed his hand and gave him a half-smile. "Yeah. I'm just mad. I'm mad at Adele, and Chip, and Mason. I wanted to talk to Mom." My throat closed and I shut my eyes, letting the balmy breeze cool my heated cheeks. Crying about it wouldn't solve my problems.

Dad slowed the cart, and I opened my eyes as he pulled up to a gate outside a large, single story building surrounded by towering metal poles. Rows of palm trees and thick Florida foliage had hidden the entire building. I missed Colorado, where people saw for miles from the high hills and mountains. It was shocking to be in a place that was all flat, so the only view you had was what was right in front of you.

A man at the gate stepped out of the booth and waved to us. Dad pulled right up.

"Jonah Booker! Adele said you'd be stopping by."

Dad grinned. "Hey, Vin. This is my daughter, Ashlyn, and this is Luca."

Vin's eyes widened. "So it's true? She came from out there?"

Dad chuckled. "Yeah. So did I, remember? Didn't you get to gawk at them at the party, like the rest of the City?"

Vin shook his head, and he gave us an embarrassed smile. "I, uh, was on duty, so I couldn't go. Sorry. We aren't used to storm people."

I shrugged. "Well, we exist."

Vin laughed, and he shoved his hands in his pockets. "Well, Adele said you could drive around the grounds, but you're not allowed to go inside, okay?"

Dad nodded. "Thanks, Vin. We won't be long. Ashlyn just wanted to see this building. She saw the pillars on the way in and had a few questions about how it works."

Vin's face became guarded. "Well, I suppose that's okay if Adele says it's okay. I mean, it's not like she can leave and sell anything to anyone. Did you hear they got Goliath to sustain a six?" Pride covered Vin's face.

"Yeah, I did. That's amazing."

"Sure is. They've been talking about that for as long as I've been alive, and they finally harvested enough energy."

Dad gave me a sideways glance, then smiled at Vin. "Well, we better go. We have to make it over to Portside soon, so I can charge this old bucket."

Vin grinned and stepped inside the booth to hit a button that opened the gate. "You got it. I hope to see you again soon, Jonah. It's been too long."

Dad shrugged. "You know how it is. Busy, busy."

Vin laughed and waved us through. "Don't I know it. Well, enjoy!"

The building wasn't remarkable. It was a white one-story building with low bushes near the walls. Beautiful rock landscaping covered the grounds with no grass. It reminded me of the landscaping in some yards in Colorado, where people designed their yards to not need any water. There weren't any windows, except at the front entrance. Small satellite dishes lined the edges of the top of the building, each pointed at one of the metal poles.

"So I take it this is Weather Production?" I asked, leaning forward to look at the poles.

Dad slowed the cart to almost a crawl. "Yep. I wish I could show you inside, but it's just a bunch of offices and screens. It would take weeks to show you all the programs they use. This will do."

"You've been inside?"

"Yeah, when I first got here. Geno, Adele's father, thought I might be a good fit for Weather Production because of my work at USHA. But I just couldn't be a part of it. It was like asking me to help develop weapons that were pointed at my family."

My heart turned over. I think I finally understood my dad. It was so frustrating to be so close to the source of the storm and not be able to do anything about it.

"What are those colored spikes at the top of the poles?" Luca asked. I leaned my head out of the cart and noticed the wavy metal parts attached to the top. They were painted in random colors.

Dad chuckled. "Those are for decoration. They don't have anything to do with anything. Those poles send signals out to the pillars."

"Is there a separate facility for harvesting energy?" I asked.

He gaped at me. "There are six. I'm surprised you knew to ask that."

I shrugged. "Well, Vin said that they harvested enough energy to bump Goliath to a six. Besides, that's what Mom does."

He slowed the cart to a stop. "What does Mom do?"

"She runs the Energy Farming department at USHA. Right?"

His face drained of color. "Your mom worked in research. When did she change jobs?"

"I don't know. I was just a kid. All I knew was that she worked at USHA until Chip told me she ran the department. That prince of a guy told me that if I didn't keep my mouth shut about what I'd learned that he'd demote her and promote, and I quote, 'a hot young intern who would be *very* grateful.'" Blech. Just saying the words gave me a nasty taste in my mouth.

Dad rubbed his face. "One thing Chip and I never agreed on was energy farming. He kept saying it was the one good thing about Goliath, and that we shouldn't be so quick to shut it down. But I thought we should apply that technology in other ways that *didn't* mean destroying large areas of land."

I sat still. This would have been a perfect time to say "I told you so," but I'm not sure it would have helped.

Luca turned in his seat. "So, how do they get the energy from the harvesting facilities here?"

Dad put the cart in gear and pulled forward. "Underground wiring. See how there's no grass around here? The wiring kills anything that grows. In fact, you'll notice that as we drive around. You'll see wide paths of rocks that lead here and out to the perimeter pillars. Those are the wire paths."

We finished our circle around the building, and Dad waved to Vin on our way out. I was sad to leave. I wanted to go inside. But I had to trust that Miri would figure out something that would help.

Dad drove for about fifteen more minutes, then pulled up to a clean, shiny building. It was the most modern building I had seen so far in the City. He pulled into a parking spot and turned, looking pleased with himself. "Guess where we are?"

I snorted. "How would I even know? And please don't say something dumb, like the library."

He grinned. "This is the Medical Facility. And we *get* to go inside."

Excitement flooded my belly. "Really? I'm allowed?"

"Yep. Plus, I need to pick up more iron tabs for us. And I have one more surprise for you inside. Uh, Luca, I guess you can come too."

I rolled my eyes, then smiled at Luca as we hopped out of the cart. Finally, I could see where Miri's miracle had taken place.

The grounds around this building were lush, divided by rock beds into large segments. Each segment had a shaded seating area and a fountain. The entire area was peaceful. Only no one was outside.

Dad caught my look. "Most people are too busy to come enjoy this place. But it's there if needed. I'm actually surprised they brought Miri to Gwen's so fast. Usually they have someone recover out at one of these spots."

We entered the building, and I was immediately hit with a cool, lavender and vanilla scented mist. I felt like I had stepped into a picture of a lobby for a spa.

Dad walked right up to the receptionist's desk and greeted the woman sitting there. "Hey, Runa. This is my daughter, Ashlyn."

Runa gasped. "Oh, Jonah, she's beautiful! I just can't believe she's here!"

For a minute, I wondered if this tour was for me, or for Dad to get a chance to show me off. He looked like he was having so much fun, though, so I guess I didn't care.

I smiled, unsure of what to say. "Um, hi. Nice to meet you."

Dad grinned. "Are we on time?"

Runa nodded. "Oh yeah. In fact, there are rooms available for all of you, if you boys want a refresher, too."

I looked at Dad. "What's a refresher?"

His eyes twinkled. "Has your mom ever taken you to a spa?"

"No way. She's way too busy. And that costs money."

"Well, this whole medical facility is essentially a spa. They have mists and pods that heal anything. And then there are the refresher rooms. They're designed for people to use on a regular basis, which will prevent the need for any of the treatment mists and pods."

I had no idea what he was talking about. "What happens in a refresher room?"

Runa laughed. "Come with me. It'll be the best thing you've done in your life, especially since you've never done one before. Boys? You coming?"

Luca looked uncomfortable, but he nodded. "Yeah, I guess. But don't tell Jack, okay?"

Dad laughed. "Men do these, too. In fact, your whole team is really due for refreshers. I'll make the appointments, and then we just need to let their supervisors know."

We followed Runa down a hall, where the lights grew dimmer. A pleasant blend of floral and fruity scents filled the air, and she stopped at a dark wooden door. "Ashlyn, this is your room. Just step inside. The computer will tell you what to do."

I looked at Dad, and he smiled. "Go. I'll see you in about thirty minutes. We'll stop for lunch after, okay?"

I pushed open the door and stepped into a darkened room. The door closed behind me.

"Welcome, Ashlyn. We're glad to have you here." A soothing voice filled the room, but no one was there.

"Hello?"

"Please, be at ease. Remove your clothes and put on the provided garments."

"What? No way."

"Please be at ease. Remove your clothes and put on the provided garments."

Okay, this robot voice would not shut up. A small bench next to the door held a set of white booty shorts and a tube top. I hoped I didn't have to leave the room in that.

I glanced around, and satisfied that I could change without being seen, did what Robot Lady asked. I folded my clothes and tucked my underwear deep into the pile, as if someone were going to come in and judge how I left my stuff.

A low hum filled the room, and the temperature immediately changed into the perfect temp. I wasn't cold or hot. It felt just right.

"Well done. Please stand with your arms slightly apart from your body. We are preparing the scan."

"What scan?"

"Please stand with your arms slightly apart from your body. We are preparing the scan."

I guess it was time to trust Dad. He said this would be good. I took a deep breath and held my arms out like a dolt. A gentle chime sounded about five seconds after I had positioned myself.

"Excellent. Scan complete. Please enter the inner door."

I admit, I was a little sad that I didn't see any lasers or light beams scanning me. I stepped through the door as commanded and entered a smaller room that held a single padded cot with a pillow.

"Please lie down on your back. You may remove the pillow if you wish."

This time I didn't question Robot Lady. Besides, I *was* pretty tired. I slept like a rock every night, but somehow I never quite felt fully rested.

"Would you like to listen to music? Classical? Jazz? New Age?"

I let out a laugh. She had weird names for music. "Uh, give me jazz, I guess."

"Excellent." The sound of a soft, soothing saxophone accompanied by the sound of gentle waves crashing on a beach filled the room as I laid down on the cot. I heard a soft hiss as the scent of ylang-ylang filled the room.

"Your refresher has begun. Relax and enjoy."

I closed my eyes, surprised at how comfortable the cot was. Without even trying, the tension drained out of my body, and I wondered why Dasha and I had never heard this type of jazz before. The music faded.

CHAPTER 12

A LOUD POUNDING WOKE me from the best nap I had ever taken. I groaned and turned on my side.

"Trig, go away."

"Ashlyn? Ashlyn, I'm going to come in, okay?" A muffled girl's voice called out, and I made myself open my eyes. I was in the refresher room, only the lights were much brighter.

Robot Lady's voice repeated over me. "Your refresher has ended. Please exit. Your refresher has ended. Please exit."

For a moment, I wanted to throw my pillow at the disembodied voice and beg for a few more minutes. But then I realized how amazing I felt. I sat up and stretched. As relaxing as the room was, I didn't need to stay in there anymore. I was ready to face anything.

"Ashlyn?"

"I'm awake! I'm coming." I hurried to the door before Runa could open it. Although she was a fellow girl, I didn't know her, and I didn't want her to see me in these skivvies.

"Oh, good. Okay, I'm leaving now so you can come out and get dressed. Can you find your way back to reception?"

"Yeah. I got it."

"Perfect. Take your time!"

I pressed my ear to the door and listened for the click of the outer door before moving into that room. The lights were bright in there too, and the room was much cooler. This place knew how to make things just uncomfortable enough to make you want to leave when your time was up.

I put on my clothes and paused for a minute, unsure what to do with the shorts and top.

"Please place the used garments on the bench and exit. We look forward to your next refresher."

I saluted the room and did as asked. Dad and Luca sat opposite each other on chairs in the lobby, looking awkward.

Luca jumped up. "Whoa, you look great."

My cheeks heated as I stopped. "What do you mean?"

Dad looked like he wanted to be upset with Luca, but he smiled at me instead. "The refresher is amazing. You don't look tired anymore. You look like an energetic, nubile eighteen-year-old."

"Nubile? Oh, gross Dad."

He laughed. "Sorry. You just look fantastic. And your hair is brown again. You look just like Mella did the last time I saw her." His eyes misted over.

I turned and glimpsed myself in the giant mirror behind Runa's desk. My mouth dropped open. He was right. I looked like I had spent hours getting a facial, and someone had done a perfect job with natural makeup. Only I knew I wasn't wearing any makeup. Even my hair was breezy and wavy. It was still short, but my natural color had been restored.

Both of them looked rested, too. Some of the lines on Dad's face were gone, and he looked like he had finally groomed himself.

"How long was I in there?" I touched my hair. For the first time since I cut and dyed it to disguise myself from Chip's goons, I felt like it might be pretty.

Runa chuckled. "Just twenty minutes. Well, I guess twenty-five. It took us a few minutes to wake you up, but that's normal for your first time."

"What happened in there?"

She looked surprised. "Just the standard things. You were infused via mist with the vitamins you're deficient in, and our lasers repaired a few minor injuries you had sustained. You know, bruising, muscle and tissue damage. That sort of thing."

"And my hair?"

She laughed. "This is what your hair looks like when it's healthy."

I shook my head. "I had no idea I had perfect beach wavy hair."

Runa looked at a loss for words, and Dad stepped in. "That's because you are used to using products and heat styling. They don't do that here."

I glanced at Luca, who still had a goofy grin on his face. "You look good, Booker."

I gave him a shy smile. "So do you."

Dad cleared his throat. "Okay, well, it's time to go. You ready for lunch?"

I rolled my eyes at Dad and reached for Luca's hand. I didn't care what Dad thought. Right then, I just wanted to be touching Luca.

Dad sighed and headed for the door. "Thanks, Runa. See you next time."

She smiled and waved. Then she called out. "Oh, wait. You forgot your iron tabs." She held out three bottles, and Dad jogged back to grab them.

"Got it. Thanks."

"Bye!"

Luca and I followed Dad out to the golf cart. Dad tucked the bottles into his pack strapped to the backseat next to Luca and sat in the driver's seat. "Ready for lunch?"

I had so many questions about the Medical Facility. "How often do people get refreshers?"

Dad puttered away and headed east. "Most go every two weeks. I don't always take the time."

I touched the skin on my arm, amazed at its softness. "Why not?"

He shrugged. "I've never been good at the self-care thing. Your mom always took care of me."

A wave of grief washed over me. I wanted to go home, but I also wanted Mom to come here. And Dasha. And even Mella. They would love the refresher. I pictured us all living here, in this tropical paradise, meeting up every week to have refreshers together. Even Mrs. Hart would love one.

The grief ebbed into anger. "Why does the City hoard its technology? Those refresher chambers could help so many people. And what they did with Miri? They could improve or even save so many lives. And instead, they choose to hide away in here and keep it all for themselves."

Dad sighed as he pulled up next to a beautiful park. "Go grab one of those tables over there in the shade. I'll get us some sandwiches."

Dad trotted over to a cafe that had a steady stream of people going in and out. They all stopped to stare at Luca and me, and I understood why Dad wanted us to eat out and away. There was no way we could talk about anything inside. Everyone would listen in.

Luca grabbed my hand and pulled me to the table. "Come on. Let's hurry."

I plopped down on the cement bench. "Hurry for what?"

He sat next to me and cupped his hand around my face. "For this." He pressed his lips to mine, and a thrill shot through my stomach.

I pulled back, surprised. "You taste like chocolate mint."

He grinned. "And you taste like watermelon. That's some refresher, isn't it?"

I smiled and grabbed his face, pulling it back to mine. I didn't know how long it would be until Dad got back, but this is what I wanted to do while we waited.

"Uh, excuse me." Dad's voice was like cold water splashing over us, and I sighed before pulling away from Luca.

Dad looked so uncomfortable that I had to laugh. "Oh, Dad. Haven't you seen anyone kiss before?"

He looked grim as he set a bag and three glass bottles of sparkling water on the table. "Not my eight-year-old baby."

I gave him a wry grin. "Well, you still haven't seen that, because I'm eighteen. Considered an adult by the state of Colorado and our nation." My throat closed as those words popped out of my mouth. Mr. Hart's words.

Dad grunted, and he handed out sandwiches. "I'm still going to need some time to remember that."

I unwrapped the sandwich and peeked inside. Cheese, tomato, and sprouts. I sighed. "Man, what I wouldn't give for a burger."

Dad chomped into his sandwich. "You'll get used to it. But let's not forget our iron pills tonight."

Luca narrowed his eyes. "What is with those pills, anyway? Nash won't let me leave work until I take them every day. It's almost like he's worried I'm going to drop dead if I take two steps away from the maintenance shed without them."

Dad took a swig of the water. "They developed them in the Med Facility to supplement what everyone is missing on the plant-based diet. Iron is one of the top deficiencies of a vegetarian."

I drank my water, delighted that it tasted like cherries. "The refreshers don't make up for that?"

"Since people only go every two weeks, they need the iron more often. I heard it was a real problem until they developed the blend about twenty years ago. Productivity had dropped significantly, because people were too tired to carry out a full day's work."

I sighed. "Man, they are obsessed with productivity around here. I guess they don't care about work life balance, do they?"

Luca still looked unconvinced. "And they think these are magic pills that help them?"

Dad shrugged. "I believe them. They know what they're doing when it comes to medical science."

We finished our sandwiches and water, and Dad took the sandwich wrappers and bottles back to the cafe for recycling. I had to admit, they had figured out a few things about waste management in here. I guessed it was because they had limited space, and their only other option would be to toss garbage out into Goliath.

Dad handed me a piece of paper once we got back into the golf cart. "Here, help me navigate. We're going to one of the Mayor Mansions, and I've never been there before."

"How am I supposed to help? I'm not from around here and I don't have my com. Would GPS even work in here?"

Dad chuckled. "There are directions on that paper. This is how they navigated in the old days. They read directions, or even looked at a paper map themselves."

"Like pirates of old," Luca said. Dad cracked up, and I smiled. Maybe Dad was finally warming up to Luca.

"Uh, okay. It says 'take Main Street to the palm row, then turn south.'" I wrinkled my nose. These directions were weird.

Dad nodded. "Got it." He headed away from the cafe, and I got caught up looking at our surroundings. We were pretty far away from the center of the City, and the buildings were farther apart. I realized I hadn't seen any houses or bungalows in a while. The road was lined with palm trees and other thick foliage, giving the sensation of driving through a tunnel.

"Doesn't anyone live out here?"

Dad shrugged. "I guess not."

"What's that?" Luca leaned over the back seat and pointed. Dad slowed the cart, and I finally saw it through the trees.

"Is that a building?" I leaned out, trying to get a better glimpse of the massive wall that seemed to be as tall as the trees.

Dad stopped. "I don't know." He looked around, but we hadn't seen anyone on this road since we left the cafe.

"Can we check it out?"

Dad looked unsure, but nodded. He pulled the cart to the side of the road in a spot that allowed him to park off the road. "Only for a minute. The note Adele gave me said the mansion is expecting us by three, and so we don't have much time."

We all jumped out of the cart and pushed our way through the dense bushes, Luca leading the way. For a minute, it felt like the bushes were pushing back on us, trying to keep us away. But I laughed to myself. That was ridiculous.

"Whoa." Luca stopped short.

"What the—" Dad's mouth dropped open.

A towering beige wall stretched almost as far as we could see in either direction. There weren't any windows or doors, just a solid wall. The color of the wall was almost identical to the trunks of the palm trees, and I was impressed that Luca had even noticed it. At first I thought there were bushes on the top of the wall that mimicked palm fronds, but I realized it was barbed wire and deadly-looking spikes.

"What is this place?" I asked.

Dad shook his head. "I have no idea. I've never spent much time on this side of town. I've only passed through to get to Greta and Yuri's."

I could see why people just pass by. From the road, if you're going along at speed, you wouldn't notice anything.

"Come on." I headed for the end of the wall.

Dad grabbed my arm. "Ashlyn, stop."

I pulled away, surprised he had grabbed me with such a firm grip. "Why? I want to see if there is anything around the corner."

Dad shook his head. "I have a bad feeling about this."

Luca folded his arms, and for a moment, he looked like his dad. I had seen that same expression on Tyler's face during the Storm Chasers meetings. The one that questioned everything and said that we deserved answers. "A bad feeling about what? We're just looking."

Dad stood firm. "Clearly, this is not something they want us looking at."

"And how do you know that? Did you know this was here?"

"No. If it was allowed, we'd all know about it."

My mouth dropped open. "Are you serious? You think that's okay? What happened to you that you are so willing to cower when they tell you to?"

Anger flashed across Dad's face. "I'll tell you what happened. I had to sit by, helpless, while powerful people held a virtual gun to my family's head. And the only way I could stop it was by doing exactly what they said, which was shutting up, putting my head down, and minding my own business in here. And it worked. It kept you all safe. And I will keep doing that until my dying breath, because that sacrifice is worth it, Ashlyn."

His outburst shocked me speechless. The actual fear in his voice squeezed my heart, and I finally realized that I would never question him again.

I looked back at Luca with pleading eyes, then turned back to Dad. "Dad, I'm sorry. I get it now. I do. Okay, we can go."

Luca let out a loud sigh. "Are you serious?"

I stepped close to him and grabbed his hand. "Yes. We can honor their privacy, okay?" I squeezed his hand and tried to communicate once more with my eyes. This time Luca seemed to catch on, and he grunted.

Luca led the way back through the thick foliage and Dad brought up the rear. I made sure he was in the back on purpose. I wanted him to know that we were going to do as he asked.

My heart pounded, though. Because while we were going to keep to Dad's schedule now, Luca and I *would* ask questions later. Dad may have had a bad feeling about the place, but I had a great feeling about it.

Whatever was behind that wall was probably the key to stopping this whole thing and going home.

CHAPTER 13

THE PALM TREE TUNNEL stretched for another two miles. Dad chattered on about legends the locals had about this stretch of road, and I tried to laugh at all of the weird quirks he pointed out. But I was as distracted as Luca was. Luca could not stop straining to see through the trees, trying to keep track of the wall.

We finally emerged from the tunnel and hit a dead end. Straight ahead in the distance was the dark, swirling mass of Goliath's eyewall. We could either go right or left.

Dad twisted his mouth. "I take it we go left? Because I always turn right here to go to Yuri's."

I checked the paper. "Yeah, left for two miles, then we should see it, I guess."

He pressed the pedal to move the golf cart, and it sputtered before responding. "Drat. We're almost out of juice. We shouldn't have stopped in the tunnel."

I patted his arm. "Don't worry. If we're almost there, we could walk, right?"

He pressed his lips together. "Yeah, but if these golf carts run out of power, it takes an extra twelve hours to charge them. And we have to be back to our side of the City by the day after tomorrow. If we're stuck here for extra time, you won't get to see everything."

I kept my mouth shut. I wasn't sure I needed to see anything else. What I wanted to spend my time doing was checking out whatever was behind that wall. "Oh. Well, we'll make it. We're almost there."

Dad gave a small smile. "You always were the optimistic one. Now, if Mella were here, she'd be fussing at me as if we were already stuck."

I laughed. "You mean Doomsday Darla? That's what Mom always used to call her. Then Trig would call her Dorksday Darla, and there would be a huge fight, and they would both end up cleaning the kitchen together for an hour."

Luca reached over the seat and squeezed my shoulder. I waited for the familiar sinking feeling of remembering my family, but this time it didn't sting so badly. I wasn't sure if that's because I was coming to terms with being stuck in here away from them, or if it's because I hadn't given up hope of seeing them again soon. Finding that wall had given me a spark. Or maybe it was still the relaxing effects of the refresher.

We weren't going as fast as we had gone before, but we finally made it around a bend, and the grounds of the Mayor's Mansion stretched out in front of us.

Dad stopped the cart and stared. "Oh, wow. This is how the other half lives, right?"

I snorted. "Half? I feel like this is the one percent. The mayor's family above all else."

He shrugged, and we puttered down the long driveway to the circle drive in front of the massive front door. A tall, thin, middle-aged woman came out the front door.

"Jonah Booker?"

Dad nodded and hopped out of the cart. "Yeah, that's me. This is Ashlyn and Luca."

For a moment, I would have almost said that her smile looked relieved. But she schooled her features and put on a professional face. Luca and I grabbed our packs and climbed

"I'm Lisha, the housekeeper. I'm so glad to have you. We don't get many visitors."

Luca folded his arms. "Oh yeah? Why's that?"

A stricken expression covered Lisha's face, as if she had no idea how to respond.

I jabbed him with my elbow. "What he means is thank you for having us."

Dad stepped up and shook Lisha's hand. "I'm sorry to be so abrupt, but I really need to charge the cart. Where can I do that?"

She gestured to the path that lead around the massive house. "Follow that gravel path. The carport is toward the back, near the pool. You can't miss it. We figured you'd need a charge, so Lev moved out a cart for you."

Dad saluted and hopped into the cart. He was really worried about that thing losing charge.

I hiked my pack up on my back. "So, who's Lev?"

Lisha blushed. "Uh, he's my husband. And the groundskeeper." I must have given her an odd look, because she giggled. "Sorry, I know I'm making it weird. We're newlyweds. We got married two months ago, so it's weird to call him my husband. But we were so used to sneaking around that I'm also not used to other people knowing about it."

I grinned. "Sneaking around?"

"Yeah. I mean, the Renwicks have always been so strict about not having any drama on the staff at their residences, so there has always been a policy against inter-staff relationships. But Lev and I have worked here together for almost ten years, and, well, sometimes you just can't deny the sparks, can you?"

Luca grabbed my hand and intertwined his fingers with mine. "No, you can't."

My cheeks warmed as Lisha's eyes twinkled. "Ooo, young love. Sorry. I love this stuff. I'm sure you can tell I'm very old, and I never thought it was going to happen to me. I mean, the Renwicks rarely match their house staff. So when Adele gave us the permission, we were thrilled."

I wrinkled my nose. "Permission? Match? What are you talking about?"

She bit her lip, as if she were worried that she had said too much. "Um, well, it's a long story. Anyway, let's go inside. I'm sure Lev will show Jonah in through the back, so we can meet him in the solarium."

The air was cool inside the house, and everything was immaculate. "So, how often do you get visitors?"

She kept a brisk walk through the cavernous halls. "The Renwicks stay here for a week or two every winter, for sure. But often one of them will pop in at random times to stay the night. They don't tell us ahead of time when that's going to happen, so we have to keep things ready at all times."

I was short of breath chasing after her. "What about other visitors?"

She slowed her pace to almost a crawl and cleared her throat. "I don't mean to be rude, but I'm not at liberty to discuss other visitors."

Luca glanced at me, then put on his most disarming smile. "Hey, no worries. We're curious about this place. We came from the mainland."

That caused her to stop next to one of the large potted bamboo palm. "I'm...I'm not allowed to talk about where you came from. Or give any information that doesn't directly relate to your stay with us. So I can tell you about dinner and where the clean towels are, but that's about it, okay?"

Her eyes were wide and filled with panic, and she rubbed the bracelet on her wrist. I studied her face and opened my mouth to ask why, but she shook her head slightly and glanced at the plant on the table.

Luca put his hand on my arm and nodded. "Of course. Sorry. Like I said, we're just curious. Can we walk the grounds later? I'd love to see more of the landscaping. I'm hoping to move from City Hall maintenance to the landscaping team, because I'm really tired of being stuck indoors." He maintained eye contact with Lisha.

She stared back and then smiled. "Of course you can. After dinner is the perfect time. You'll want to watch the sun set behind Goliath."

Was I being paranoid, or was Lisha trying to tell us that the house was bugged? I gave Luca a look, and he pressed his lips together, shook his head, and tugged on my hand to follow Lisha into the next room, which I guessed was the solarium. It was basically a sun room, the walls and ceiling made up of glass. The room overlooked the backyard, which was a stunning panoramic view of the area. The grass and flowers were arranged in a patchwork quilt pattern, with ten-foot wide gravel paths criss-crossing all the sections. No structure sat between the house and Goliath's eyewall, several miles away.

"Amazing, isn't it?" Lisha asked, staring at the storm. "The raw power is incredible."

I snorted. "Yeah. Although I'd use words like 'terrifying' and 'deadly,' but I guess you can say incredible."

Lisha shot me a look, then moved to a set of glass French doors. "Oh, but you should see it from outside." She pulled open the doors, stepped through and waited for us to follow. "Come see it from the gazebo. I think that's where Jonah is, anyway."

I glanced at Luca and followed her outside. The storm looked the exact same.

Lisha walked about twenty feet down the path, then turned and looked at us. Luca shrugged and followed. Once we reached her, though, she did not continue on to the gazebo next to the elaborate pool.

"This is a dead spot." She lowered her voice, and we had to lean close to hear her.

"What?" I asked.

She motioned with her hand to keep my voice down. "This is one of the few spots that surveillance can't pick anything up on. Go up behind the pool shed after dinner. But don't say a word when you get there. I'll meet you there and take you to Lev and my secret place where we can talk."

She suddenly started walking again. When she was just a few feet away, she spoke in a normal voice, as if we had been talking the whole time. "Let me know what your favorite flavor of sparkling water is, and I'll make sure the pool bar is stocked."

I glanced at Luca, then hurried after her. "We're not here that long. I don't want you to go to any trouble."

She grinned. "It's no trouble. Seriously." She hurried down to the pool and pressed a button hidden under the rock bench next to the pool. A sudden rush sounded as a waterfall turned on, turning the still pool into a tropical paradise. She beckoned us closer to the waterfall.

"If you stand right here, the sound of the waterfall makes it so you can't be overheard. I can't stay here for very long, or they'll get suspicious."

I was getting exasperated. "Who? Adele?"

She nodded. "The whole Renwick family. They track my movements. If they don't hear me within a certain amount of time, I get docked."

My mouth dropped open. "Are you a prisoner?"

She laughed. "No, of course not. I'm so happy this is my job. Most of the time, we get to do whatever we want. But they do track us, especially when there is someone else in the house. And I know the only reason they let Lev and me get married is because they've determined that they can trust us. I can't break that trust. Not yet."

Luca grinned at the waterfall. "Brilliant."

Lisha's face became serious. "You remember where to meet me after dinner?"

I nodded. "Behind that shed on the hill over there?"

Her expression brightened, and she moved away from the waterfall. I followed her while Luca dragged a lounge chair close to the waterfall. Lisha watched him, then motioned for him to move it a little closer. He grinned and pushed the chair, then walked across the deck to grab another.

"So, will you need anything else?" Lisha asked, her professional voice back in place.

I shrugged. "Um, just my dad."

"Oh, Jonah's your dad?" She kept her tone conversational enough that I wasn't sure if she already knew this.

"Yeah. Do you know where he is?"

She grinned. "I bet he got dragged into some boring conversation about golf carts with Lev. I'll go get him. You guys hang out here for a while, okay?"

I smiled at her, grateful for the gift she had given us: a chance to talk near the waterfall, in private.

"Thanks, Lisha."

"My pleasure. Dinner will be in a couple of hours, but I'll come get you. Relax and enjoy!" She gave a brief nod, then clipped away from the pool.

Luca was already stretched out on one of the lounge chairs, so I settled next to him.

"Well, what do you think?" I asked. I had to raise my voice quite a bit to be heard over the waterfall, and for a minute I wondered if I was talking too loud.

He didn't seem concerned. "I think we're about to find out some things that could help."

I stared at the beautiful pool, the calm setting a sharp contrast to the wicked storm in the background. "Do you think she knows anything about that wall?"

He put his hands behind his head and leaned all the way back. "I think she knows everything about that wall."

I followed Luca's lead and tried to not get my hopes up. Just because we might get information didn't mean we'd be able to act on it. I took a deep breath and reminded myself to settle into the long game. Moving on anything too quickly could lead to mistakes, and there really wasn't anywhere to hide in the eye. If the Renwicks had this level of surveillance at the mansion, where else did they watch?

CHAPTER 14

Dad laughed at the look on my face. "You like it, don't you?"

I stared at my plate in disgust. I didn't want to admit it to anyone, but I really did like it. "Yeah, fine. I guess."

He stabbed his fork into the most delicious salad I had ever had. "See? It grows on you."

I scooped up the mix of nuts, cheese, and greens and shoved the bite in my mouth. There was something about that dressing. I didn't even miss the meat.

"Lisha, tell the cook we loved this," I said as she entered the room with another basket of the softest sourdough bread I had ever had.

She grinned. "I will. She'll be happy to hear it. Can I get you guys anything else?"

Luca leaned back as he pushed his plate away. "No way. I never thought I'd be full after salad and bread, but here I am."

"No room for ice cream?"

His face fell. "I didn't know about dessert."

Her eyes shone. "How about ice cream after a walk? You wanted to see Goliath at sunset, right?"

A thrill shot through my stomach. "That's right. When is sunset?"

"In about twenty minutes, so go ahead." She made eye contact with me and gave the slightest nod as she picked up Luca's plate.

I pushed back from the table at the same time as Luca. My heart sank as Dad did the same.

"Oh, we're going on a walk?"

This was the problem with never being allowed to see any of my friends, and never having any alone time with Luca. I didn't know if we should bring Dad in on this. He had already made it clear that he was willing to toe the line and do what Chip and Adele told him, because it would keep Mom and everyone else safe. I didn't blame him for that at all. But how far would he take it? Would he try to stop anything the Storm Breakers would try to do?

Because the bottom line was, I didn't agree with him, and I didn't want to make the same choices as he did.

Thankfully, Dad seemed to pick up on my hesitation. "Uh, because I'd rather stay here. I didn't get the chance you guys did to hang out around the pool. I was too busy with Lev talking about golf carts."

My heart swelled. "Are you sure?"

He chuckled. "Yeah. I'm sure I can see the sunset just fine from the pool."

I jumped up and ran around the table to kiss him on the cheek. "Thanks, Daddy. We'll be back soon."

He winked at me, then stood up. "Oh, hang on. It's iron tab time. But I left them in my bag in my room."

Lisha stepped into the room with a small silver plate. "I've got them for you here. Does anyone need water?"

Luca narrowed his eyes, but reached for his tab and swallowed it. I hadn't thought anything of it before, but he was right. They were obsessed with these iron tabs around here.

Dad swallowed his tab, then headed out of the dining room toward the library Lisha had shown us earlier. Luca smiled, and we headed out the door.

I reached for Luca's hand as we stepped onto the gravel path that lead toward the shed. Luca stopped and squatted down.

"These stones are hot. I can feel it through my shoes."

I reached down and felt the radiating heat before I even touched any of the gravel. "Maybe they absorb the heat from the sun?"

"Maybe. But it's not that hot here, and it's not like we're that close to the sun."

I studied the path. It stretched from the house out toward Goliath. "I bet it's the power lines. Remember what Dad said? It's how they transfer energy harvested from the storm."

Luca took a few steps down the path. "So, do you think the harvesting facilities are out that way?"

I shrugged. "Probably. But I doubt those are on the tour."

He looked conflicted for a moment, then turned back to me. "Okay. We can see them next time." His voice was loud, and he grinned at me, and I realized he said that for the benefit of anyone who might be listening. I covered my mouth with my hand to muffle my laugh.

We tried to make conversation about the grounds for the sake of the listening ears, but we could hardly do it without laughing. When we got close to the shed, Luca wiggled his eyebrows at me, then shouted, "Wanna make out?"

I gave a loud, "Yes!" and we ran the last few yards around the back of the shed, cracking up the whole time. Lisha stood with her arms folded, a huge smile on her face.

"Real smooth, guys."

I shrugged. "We wanted to give Adele a show."

She laughed, and her face looked both relaxed and eager, a surprising difference from the polished, professional look she kept at the house. "Adele doesn't have time to listen, but I know what you mean. Anyway, I only have a few minutes, but there are some things you should know."

I glanced at Luca. "Good, because we have so many questions. Like what's behind that wall a couple of miles from here?"

Lisha shook her head. "That will take too long. And it doesn't matter yet. But what you need to know is about the iron tabs."

Luca nodded. "They're not iron, are they?"

"I mean, they have iron in them. But it's not their primary function."

He clenched his fist and grinned. "I knew it."

My heart pounded. "What *is* their primary function, then?"

Lisha looked around, then glanced at her bracelet. "They're essentially sleeping tabs. Have you noticed how hard you sleep?"

I tried to think. "I guess not. I've always been a heavy sleeper, though."

"Well, these are designed to really knock you out. Everyone in the City takes them, everyone is dead to the world between ten p.m. and six a.m."

I didn't understand what she was saying. "Okay, so?"

Frustration filled her face. "So no one knows what's going on during those hours."

Luca took a step closer. "But you do?"

Lisha pressed her lips together and looked like she was struggling for words. "You guys are going to have to figure out a lot of things on your own, so that I can honestly tell them I didn't tell you. But you guys are smart. I mean, you got into the eye, which no one is supposed to do. Not the way you came in, anyway."

My mouth dropped open. "What do you mean, not the way we came in?"

Lisha held her hands up. "I just wanted to tell you about the iron tabs. Also, the iron tab I gave you today is *not* like the ones you've been taking. If you'd like clean ones, leave your bottles next to your bathroom sink in the morning before breakfast. You'll have new bottles by the time you pack up to leave."

I wasn't happy that Lisha had given me a new tab. "What will this new tab do?"

She raised an eyebrow. "It will give you iron and only iron. And trust me, you'll understand the difference tonight." She checked her bracelet, which I finally realized was a watch. The old-school technology of this place surprised me every time. "I have to go, or they'll know I'm not at home."

Luca's face darkened. "They watch your home, too?"

She shrugged. "We're pretty sure there are no bugs inside, but we know there are cameras monitoring our doors, so they can track when we come and go. I'd tell you that our cottage is a safe place to talk, but I couldn't get you inside without them seeing, so this will have to work."

I sighed. "Are we ever going to get straight answers about anything?"

Lisha set her mouth. "Now that you're here, I hope so. You have no idea how great it is that you made it through the storm. We've been waiting for this day."

"Who has?"

She flashed a smile and backed away. "We can chat again tomorrow. I'll see you at breakfast. Sleep 'well.'" She made air quotes with her fingers when she said the word "well." She turned and walked briskly over the hill and out of sight.

I growled. "Don't you miss the days where people just answered your questions? Or if you wanted to know something, you just looked it up on your tech pad?"

Luca laughed and reached for my hand. "You and I grew up very differently. No one ever answered my questions. Or my dad's. We had to learn how to dig out everything and find the truth."

I let him lead me back to the warm gravel path. "How did you not go crazy?"

"Well, people called us crazy. But we just knew the answers were out there. And it was worth our time, effort, and reputation to find them. And look where we are." He stopped and pointed at the sky that had turned a brilliant shade of orange as the rays of the setting sun bounced off the low-lying clouds that had escaped from Goliath's borders. "We're in the eye. Where there are people and a thriving City. Just like we always thought there was."

I stood frozen. He was right. I always knew Dad was alive, and I never let anyone stop me from looking until I found the answer. "Yeah, but most of the people we asked out there *didn't* know, so it wasn't their fault. But in here, everyone does, and no one is sharing."

Luca was silent as he watched the colors fade. "You know what? I don't think everyone knows what is going on. Especially if what Lisha said about the iron tabs is true. What else are the people given that keep them in the dark?"

My blood ran cold as I remembered the refresher. What if that was another tactic to dumb us down? Was I even thinking clearly?

We had little to say on our way back down to the pool. I was too busy trying to figure out if I had missed anything obvious.

Dad sat in a lounge chair with a book in his hand. He didn't even look up as we approached. "How was the lover's stroll?"

I rolled my eyes and plopped down on the end of his chair. "Gross, Dad."

Luca dragged a chair close and sat down. "It was enlightening."

Dad shut his book. "What does that mean?"

I gave Luca a warning glance. We weren't close enough to the waterfall to have our conversation masked.

Luca grinned. "The sky? Didn't you watch? It 'enlightened' with a shade of orange we had never seen."

Dad groaned, then chuckled. "Ooo, good dad joke there, son."

My mouth dropped open, and I shook my head. "Never laugh at bad jokes, Dad."

I studied the sky, now a darkening shade of gray. "Dad? Are you sure you know what's in those iron tabs you make us take?"

Dad sighed and sat up, putting his feet on the ground. "It's a vitamin blend. They help us sleep at night and give us energy during the day."

I turned and studied his face. "Have you always been a heavy sleeper?"

He laughed. "Yeah. Your mom hated it. I never once heard any of you cry. When Mella was born, your mom accused me of faking it, until one night she had her in bed with us and Mella puked all over me. It took your mom a solid minute of shaking me to get me to wake up. After that, she just accepted it."

I let out the laugh he was expecting, but I was a little disappointed. How was I going to figure out if Lisha was telling the truth about the iron tabs?

"And you've never had any weird side effects from them?"

Dad studied my face. "Honey, you've been taking them for two weeks now. Have *you* experienced anything odd?"

I closed my eyes and tried to think. I wished I could put a finger on anything; a headache or body ache that wasn't typical, or some twitch or hiccup that appeared out of nowhere. But I couldn't. Dad was right; over the last few weeks, my health had been improving, and that refresher that morning seemed to be the cherry on top. I felt fantastic. But then something occurred to me.

"What time is it?"

Dad checked his watch. "A little after eight."

I sat still, trying to assess how I felt. "Hmm. I'm not sleepy at all."

"So?"

"The only difference I can think of is, since I got here, I am ready to go to bed not long after dinner."

Dad shrugged. "Well, you're not used to working a full-time job. I know you had school and everything, but working full time is a whole different beast. There's a mental load that most kids aren't aware of."

Luca leaned forward. "It's the same for me. I thought it was because I walk a million miles a day all over that dang City Hall for maintenance."

Dad spread his hands. "See? You're just ready for bed after a long day. And today, we didn't work, so you're not sleepy."

I sighed. "Yeah, okay."

"So, no weird side effects for you, then?"

"No, I guess not."

Luca shook his head. "Me either."

Dad smiled and lounged back in his chair again. "Just relax, guys. This is one of the nicest places you'll stay in the City. Let's enjoy it, okay?"

I glanced at Luca, and he shrugged at me before getting up and heading to the pool bar. The dark wall cloud of Goliath slowly disappeared with the darkening sky, and then we all gasped as the lightning show started.

"Now, this is what I'm talking about. Maybe they'll let me work here," Dad said, a wide grin on his face.

I was starting to understand why everyone was so willing to look the other way at the weird things that happened in this City. They all felt good, and there were some spectacular views. Oh, and there was a massive, deadly storm surrounding them.

I stood to get my own lounge chair. Might as well enjoy the show.

Chapter 15

I woke with a start and jumped out of bed. My heart was pounding in serious fight-or-flight mode, like the first time I saw a tornado funnel drop out of the sky when Luca and I were flying over the Disaster Zone.

My room was dark and still. The ceiling fan was stirring the air, and the sweet fragrance of wet grass wafted in through the cracked window. Goliath's light show flickered silently on the horizon.

"Ashlyn?" Luca called through my closed door, making me jump again.

I hurried across the massive room and threw open the door, shielding my eyes from the hall light. "What? Are you okay?"

He stepped into my room and clutched my arms, as if checking for injury. "I'm okay. Are you?"

Dad rushed to my door, frowning when he saw me and Luca. "What's going on? What happened?"

I tried to swallow, but my mouth had gone dry. I shook my head. "I don't know. Why are you guys up? I mean, I woke up completely freaked out, but I have no idea why."

Luca studied my face. "You didn't hear that?"

"Hear what?"

"That massive boom. It rattled the whole house. I felt it in my chest. For a second I thought it was an earthquake of some kind, but I don't think it lasted long enough to be an earthquake."

Dad rubbed the back of his neck. "All I know is that I'm awake. Then Luca shouted your name, and the light was on."

I took a deep breath and tried to calm my shaking hands. I was most unnerved at the fact that my body was acting terrified. "Did Luca's yelling wake you up?"

Luca pulled me into a side hug, rubbing my arms. "I wasn't yelling. But I thought that something blew up in your room or something."

My heart slowed down. Luca smelled good, which surprised me. He must have showered before bed, because he smelled like lemons and eucalyptus. My cheeks warmed as he glanced at what I was wearing. We had slept in the same storm shelters for a week, but I slept in the long-sleeved tees and joggers that I wore under our rain jumpsuits. It was much warmer in the City, so Cyra had given me a pair of shorts and a cropped T-shirt to wear to bed. I was thankful that I wore my sports bra.

Dad cleared his throat, clocking the fact that Luca was checking me out. Luca's face turned an adorable shade of pink, and he stepped away.

I wrapped my arms around myself and tried my best to not appear as self-conscious as I felt. "I didn't hear anything. I was just suddenly awake, and my heart was pounding, and I didn't know why."

"Well, I guess we should go back to bed," Dad said.

I sighed. "There's no way I can go to sleep now. What time is it?"

Dad chuckled. "It's a little after midnight. Am I the only one who wears a watch?"

I scowled. "Back home, the screens on the walls tell us the time. No one wears watches anymore."

"I want to check out outside," Luca said.

I nodded. "That's a good idea. Maybe something happened out there."

Dad crossed his arms. "Are you going to get a sweatshirt or something?"

I rolled my eyes. "Yes, Father. I'll also put on shoes, even though you didn't tell me to." I wasn't going to tell him I wanted a sweatshirt anyway, because I was unnerved at them seeing my stomach.

We all went our separate ways and put on things to go outside, then met in the dark, cavernous front entry way. Luca had grabbed a flashlight, and we followed him out to the front of the house.

A half moon gave a bit of light, but the grounds of the property were almost pitch black. The dark shapes of the palm trees were the only thing I could make out as I looked back toward the road. Dad, Luca, and I spread out in different directions, looking around. Dad headed down the path that lead to the golf cart shed, and Luca went the opposite direction.

I walked down the main driveway toward the entrance to the property. I thought the little rise that we had come over might give a nice overview. However, not all the adrenaline had left my system, so I was still jumpy. A crunching sound made me freeze, and I realized it was me walking on the gravel driveway.

I rolled my eyes at myself and turned to go tell Luca how ridiculous I was being when a low rumble filled the air. I whirled around, trying to pinpoint the sound as it quickly grew louder, then covered my ears when it exploded into a bone-shattering boom.

An orange glow grew above the palms beyond the main gate. Luca and Dad ran up next to me, and this time I reached for Dad's hand. Some primal instinct took over, and I just wanted my dad.

Luca pointed. "Isn't that where that wall is?"

All words and speculation died away as the orange fire of a rocket rose into the night sky. It climbed higher than anything I had ever seen, getting smaller and smaller, before seeming to turn and head north, away from us.

The night was dark and silent again. We stood for a few minutes, straining to see anything else in the pitch black.

Dad pulled his hand away from mine and checked his watch. "It's twelve-thirty."

"So, thirty minutes since the last one," Luca said.

"What are they doing?" I asked.

"I don't know," Dad replied. "I've never heard anything about anything being launched. Ever."

Lisha's words came back to me. "Because you've always been sleeping."

I felt more than saw Dad turn to me. "What do you mean?"

Things clicked into place. "Lisha said the iron tabs everyone takes were sleeping tabs. I think they're designed to keep people in the deepest part of sleep, where they aren't easily woken, so they can do whatever they want at night."

"When did Lisha say this?" he demanded. "Why didn't you say anything?"

I threw my hands up. "Because you let yourself be steamrolled, Dad. You don't seem willing to ask questions or do what it takes to get out of here. And I get it." I grabbed his hand and tried to see his face in the dark. "You did what you had to to keep us safe. But I'm not so willing to just meekly join this weird society. I want to go *home*. And I want to tell the world what Chip and Adele are doing with this storm. And so I'm going to do what it takes to figure out a way out of here."

My heart pounded and my eyes filled with tears, just like it did when I was a little kid and I confessed something to Dad that would get me in trouble. I hated that here I was, eighteen years old, and still worried about getting in trouble with my dad. I was beyond that now.

Luca stepped closer to me. "That's what's behind that wall. A launch site. But what are they launching?"

I laughed, incredulous. "They aren't working on it. They've *done* it."

Dad folded his arms. "You aren't making any sense."

I shook my head, still chuckling. "Mason said that Chip told him that the Air Force was working with the Space Force on a way to get into the Eye, by going up and over it. I'm sure it was Chip's way of keeping Mason in line by dangling a carrot and getting Mason to do what he wants, which is taking the Space Force track of the Air Force Academy. But of course, he didn't tell Mason that they've already done it."

"Mason is trying to get in here?" Luca asked in a quiet voice. I recognized that voice. It was the voice of insecurity, and the one that shouted in my ear the loudest whenever I saw Miri and Luca together.

I reached for his hand and intertwined my fingers with his. "I doubt it. His mom would never let him. Also, I don't care. Seriously. I don't care what he does." I wasn't sure what else to say to reassure him. I was just happy that it was the truth. I didn't care what Mason did. Luca tightened his grip, and I took that as a good sign.

Dad walked away from us toward the dark road. For a minute, I wasn't sure what he was doing. Was he just walking away? But he turned back and came back.

"I'm in."

I tried to read his face in the dark. "In what?"

"In whatever you guys are doing. You're right, Ash. It's time to leave. There has to be a way to get out of here. But we have to do it in a way that keeps your mom and siblings safe. Okay?"

Luca squeezed my hand, but I'm not sure he meant to. I think he was just getting excited. "Yes! Finally."

I laughed, dropped Luca's hand, and ran to wrap my arms around Dad's middle. "Really?"

Dad wrapped me in a hug and pressed his cheek to my hair. "It might take a while. We have to come up with a good plan."

I pushed back. "Well, the first step is to get different iron tabs. Lisha said she'd replace our bottles with ones she has. We need to give them to people so they can stop being drugged into a stupor each night."

He shook his head. "No, we have to be careful. You can't trust everyone. The first step is trying to figure out who we *can* trust."

"Well, Lisha, for starters."

"I hope so." He sounded skeptical.

The low rumble started again, and we turned to watch another rocket shoot into the atmosphere.

"Dad, Lisha gave us the right tabs."

"But why? I mean, what did she have to gain?"

Luca chuckled. "You sound like my dad. He would have liked you."

My heart turned over, and I reached for Luca's arm. "What would your dad have done? I mean, he gave me a hard time for the longest time. How would he vet people?"

Luca snorted. "I don't know how to in here. Jonah, is there anyone you trust?"

Dad was quiet for a long time. So long that my excitement over our plan began to fizzle.

I sighed. "Let's go back to bed. You think about it, Dad. You'll come up with someone tomorrow. Hopefully they're done with the launches, so we can get some sleep."

"They are." A voice from the darkness startled us, and Luca and Dad both jumped in front of me, as if they were ready to fight someone off.

"Who's there?" Dad shouted.

"Shhh." Two figures walked toward us from the direction of the main road, and Luca turned his flashlight on them.

I sighed. "It's Lisha, Dad. And I'm guessing that's Lev."

Lisha nodded. "Can you turn off that light? It's better if it's not on."

Luca grunted. "Sorry. But not sorry, because sneaking up on us like that was not cool."

I crossed my arms. "I have questions."

Lisha chuckled. "I'm sure you do."

"First, is it safe to talk here?"

"Yes. We're so glad you came out this way. There aren't audio bugs out here, just cameras along the fence."

My heart dropped. We were total idiots for bringing out the flashlight. "So they know we're out here?"

"Probably not," Lev said. "It's not like they have someone monitoring screens every minute. As far as we can tell, it's more of a check in thing."

Dad stepped forward. "Can you please catch me up? What are you talking about?"

I sighed in exasperation. "Short story—this whole place is bugged, and Lisha gave us new iron tabs. That's all we know, because Lisha wouldn't tell us anything earlier."

"Sorry about that," she said. "I wasn't sure if we could trust you. We needed to see what you would do when the launches woke you up."

I stepped closer to her, trying to see her face in the dark. "What do you mean, what we would do? Wouldn't anyone come outside to check it out?"

She shook her head. "Nope. We've tested a few visitors before. Most people have been conditioned to not question anything. If they hear a loud boom in the night, they figure that Weather Production is working on something, and go back to sleep."

"But you guys are exactly what we've been hoping for," Lev said, excitement in his voice. "I mean, of course you are. But we needed fresh blood, I guess you could say."

"Are you telling us there's a group of people in here who want to shut down the storm?" Anger flared in my chest. "Then why haven't you done it? Because Dad could have gone home years ago, and I wouldn't have had to give up my senior trip to come get stuck here."

Lisha put a hand on my shoulder. "We're a tiny group that has been trying to help people see the truth for years. But people haven't been given a good reason to shut it down. I mean, they're pretty comfortable in here. And it's easy to ignore the world outside the storm. Out of sight, out of mind. But having an entire group of people who came from outside? That's hard to ignore."

"But mostly, we need willing bodies," Lev said. "We think we know how to shut down the storm, but we need seven different teams. There are only about ten of us. And, ah, most aren't in the best shape. But if everyone from your group joins us, we'll have what we need."

Excitement built in my chest. "There are eight of us. Well, nine, because I'm sure Cyra is up for anything. What do we need to do?"

Lev sighed. "We have to shut down Weather Production and the perimeter laser stations. At the exact same time."

CHAPTER 16

I COVERED MY ENTIRE face to hide a massive yawn. For just a second, I wished it was yesterday, the day I had taken the City-issued iron pill and had my refresher. I felt so good yesterday. Today I was exhausted. Almost too tired to appreciate how adorable Luca looked, with his hair sticking straight out on one side and a sleepy look on his face.

"How did everyone sleep?" Lisha asked as she breezed into the dining room, where we were slowly eating eggs and toast. Her voice sounded too bright and chipper for someone who had stood outside on the dark lawn with us until three o'clock.

I scowled at her, and she gave a slight wink and a wide smile. She was well-practiced in putting on the best show for the surveillance.

I sat up straighter and pasted a smile on my face. "It was the most relaxing night I've ever had."

Dad and Luca stared at me as if I had lost my mind.

I bit back a laugh. "Dad, can we just stay here today? Hang out by the pool? I mean, how much more is there to see in the City, anyway?"

He leaned back and smiled. "I guess that could work. We don't have to be home until tomorrow afternoon. Although I was going to show you the energy harvesters."

I was so proud of him for picking up on what I was trying to say. I would much rather spend the day here with Lisha and Lev, because we didn't get anywhere making a plan last night. We needed more information about the rest of the team, and we needed solid action steps to take back with us.

Lisha paused in the doorway. "No, you can't stay."

My heart sank, and I tried to read her eyes.

"Why not?" Dad asked. "Adele said we could stay at any of the mansions. Why can't we just stay here?"

Lisha's eyes were wide. "You haven't seen the farmland on the north side of the city. It's where we get all our eggs. You'll want to see that."

Luca wrinkled his nose. "A chicken farm? Those are disgusting."

"Not in the City," Lisha said, panic filling her eyes. "You have to go. Trust me. Plus, Miko is expecting you. He runs the farm. I already told him you were coming. And Lev has your golf cart charged and ready to go."

I stared at her. "Are you sure?"

A wide smile replaced the panic. "Trust me. This is not something you want to miss. And since you only have a day left before you have to be back, you don't want to waste it here."

I sighed. "Okay. When will we see you again, though?"

"Aw, you're sweet. I'm sure we'll see each other again sometime." She wiggled her eyebrows. "Once you're finished, you can grab your packs from your room. I'll meet you out front." With that, she whisked herself out of the room.

Luca shoved his last bite of eggs in his mouth, then pushed away his plate. "I guess that's our invitation to get out of here."

Lisha popped her head back into the dining room. "Oh, and I'm so sorry, but I just mopped the front hall, so I'll need you to use the back hall to the guest wing. Just go through that door and take your third left. I'm so sorry for the inconvenience." Her voice sounded apologetic, but her eyes were bright.

We all gave each other a shrug, and Dad and I picked up the pace to finish our breakfasts. Luca led the way, and we walked wordlessly through a door that we thought lead to the kitchen and found ourselves in the back hall of the mansion. It was dimly lit and bare, clearly not part of the usual tour.

An open doorway on the right showed the massive kitchen. Out of curiosity, I poked my head in, and my jaw dropped at the sight of a flash cooker and in-wall coffee barista. They were more modern than anything I had seen at Cyra's house. This mansion was one of the key benefactors of the shipments of supplies that USHA sent.

I turned to Luca and Dad to say something about them, but Luca held his finger to his lips, and I clapped my hand over my mouth. I had almost forgotten the bugs. Then I heard the noise of a news app and leaned back into the kitchen.

On the wall next to the door was a wall screen, like what we had at home. It *was* a news app playing. I yanked Dad and Luca into the kitchen. Dad's eyes bugged out when he saw the screen. We froze as Chip appeared on the screen, clearly at a press conference. The banner at the bottom of the screen said "USHA Director Addresses Hurricane Breach."

Thank you for allowing me to speak today. Yes, I can confirm that a team has indeed made it safely to the eye of Goliath. The Storm Chasers, the group you know to be rogue terrorists, kidnapped Ashlyn Booker to use as collateral for safe passage through the Disaster Zone. While the team arrived unharmed, I am sad to announce that Hurricane Goliath is now at a Category Six, with winds holding steady around two-hundred miles per hour. This has made the eyewall unbreachable, from the outside or the inside. I'm sure you can imagine that communications with the team trapped in the eye are now non-existent because of these weather conditions. We pray that God has mercy on their souls, and that they are able to somehow find a way to survive in an alien landscape. USHA will continue to work tirelessly to develop technologies that might some day let us reach our lost citizens.

I'd also like to take this time to publically acknowledge my relationship with Ashlyn's mother, Livvy Booker. The entire Booker family has become near to my heart, and I am as heartbroken at the loss of Ashlyn as they are. I thank you ahead of time for respecting our privacy as we come to terms with this situation. I won't stop working to bring Ashlyn home to us, safe and sound.

I had to swallow the bile that rose in my throat as I watched Chip try to garner sympathy for himself. Dad's face was furious.

"Emmy, did you turn off the screen?" Lisha's voice echoed down the hall. "You know you can't have that on when guests are in the house."

We understood Lisha's warning and hurried back to our rooms. My bed had already been stripped, and my bag sat on the dresser, packed but still open.

I shook my head. How did Lisha have time to do all of that? I hadn't seen any other staff working at the mansion. Maybe she had another secret tablet that was a caffeine pill or something.

I used my en suite bathroom one more time, then went to close my bag. Two bottles of pills and a paper were tucked on top. I glanced around the room, hoping that I just looked like I was trying to make sure I hadn't forgotten anything, then opened the note without pulling it too far out to hide it from any cameras.

Ashlyn,

You can trust Miko. He'll introduce you to the rest of the team. Tell him what we talked about last night. I'll see you soon.

Lisha

P.S. The blue tabs are an organic energy blend. Just take one. I didn't want to talk about them out loud, but they'll help take the edge off any fatigue. The Renwicks use them, but don't know that we do.

I glanced at the bottle. Mella would die if she knew how many things I was putting in my mouth without fully understanding what it was. But Lisha seemed to do fine. I decided it was worth whatever consequence might happen and quickly swallowed one.

I hurried out of the house. Dad and Luca were waiting in the golf cart. I handed my pack to Luca and climbed into the front seat. They both looked like little boys in a toy store.

"What's goin' on, fellas?" I asked.

Luca grinned. "Look what Lev gave us." He reached over and patted a small, black, metal box that sat next to Dad. It didn't appear to have any kind of opening.

"It's a bug jammer," Dad said.

"So we can talk," Luca chimed in.

I glanced at the box. "Is it on?"

Luca nodded, and the sob that I was choking back erupted. "Good. Because, Dad, do you understand about Chip now?"

Dad's knuckles turned white as he gripped the steering wheel. "Yeah. Ash, I'm sorry I doubted you. I promise we'll get out of here. Because I owe that guy a black eye."

I wiped my eyes and settled into my seat as we puttered away from the house. I looked back, but neither Lisha nor Lev were anywhere to be seen. I was a little disappointed.

Dad passed through the gates and turned right instead of left. I was disappointed about that too. I wanted to drive by the wall again to see if we could find any way in.

Luca leaned over the seat. "I have something that will cheer you up. I found this in my pack when I got my bag." He held out a paper map.

I tried to make sense of it. "Whoa. Is that the City?"

"Lisha left me a note and said it was an old map of Orlando. Look, we're here. That area right there was an airport. I think that's where they're launching rockets."

That reminded me. I reached into my bag and pulled out the bottle of blue tabs. "Lisha gave me a present, too. They're energy pills. Want one?"

Luca gave a sigh of relief. "Yes, please. That one night of little sleep about killed me. Is this what it feels like to be old, Jonah?"

Dad grunted. "I don't know, son, because I'm not old yet. Give me one of those pills, Ash. Darn, Lisha didn't give *me* any presents."

I handed him a tab and a bottle of water. "Lev gave you that jammer. So it was Christmas for all of us."

Luca studied the map. "I think he gave me this to show what that launch site could be. But I'm not sure what else we could use this for."

"Does it say where this chicken farm is?" Dad asked. "I've never been to the farms."

I pulled out Lisha's note. "Lisha said that Miko can be trusted. And that he knows where the rest of the team is."

He nodded. "I figured that's why she was so insistent that we head that way."

I let my mind wander as Dad drove along. I was still pretty tired, and I figured the energy pill hadn't kicked in yet. There wasn't much around this part of the City, just random standalone buildings. I guess it made sense; we were pretty close to the edge of the City, which meant the towering eyewall of Goliath felt as if it were bearing down on us. You'd have to have nerves of steel to live this close to the swirling mass.

"Where do your friends live? Because it doesn't look like anyone lives out here."

Dad gestured to the northeast of us. "That way. This side of the City is where the waste recycling takes place, so not many people live out here."

"You know what I can't figure out?" Luca asked. "Why did Adele send us to that mansion? You know, with it being so close to the launch site?"

I snorted. "Arrogance. She's so sure that her iron tabs work it didn't matter. I don't think she counted on us using our eyes to look through the trees."

Luca had his hand across the backseat, and was playing with the ends of my hair. I shifted a little so that his fingers would brush my neck every once in a while. He noticed and started to play with my earlobe. My cheeks warmed.

"I don't know if I would call it arrogance, but I'm sure she was confident in those iron tabs," Dad said. "I mean, I don't think it matters where you are in the City. They can't hide those launches. Oh, here's where we turn for the farm."

We turned down a long drive that circled a large lake. Almost instantly, the earthy scent of the air was replaced by the pungent stench of chickens. I gagged. "Oh, gross."

Dad laughed. "Come on. It's the smell of money."

My mouth dropped open. "What does that mean?"

"It's something my grandpa used to say. Of course, that was about cows. You know he lived out on the ranches of northeastern Colorado. Talk about a smell."

I took another tentative sniff. "It smells like Ousley." I had almost forgotten about the livestock the people of the Ousley garage had on one of their levels. Obviously, if you were going to survive in a contained society, you needed chickens to do it.

Luca leaned forward. "Oh yeah. How come it smells so much worse here, though? Those chickens were inside, and these are outside."

I couldn't see any chickens because of the large ferns that lined the gravel paths on the property, but I could sure hear them. Dad pulled up in front of a tall, white farmhouse that looked like it belonged in another time. The door to the house banged open, and an old man in honest-to-goodness denim overalls stepped out.

"You the outsiders?" he hollered. *Hollered.* It was the only way to describe it.

I burst out laughing. "Yeah, we are."

He bounced down the steps, which surprised me since he looked to be about a hundred years old. "I'm Miko. Boy, am I glad to see you. Here, son, drive that cart around the side here and plug her in. Those confounded things have to be charged all the time, it's a wonder they can make it ten feet."

Luca and I hopped out while Dad did what he was told. A much younger looking woman came out the door. "Pops, give them a break. I'm sure their cart has enough charge."

"Why risk it?" Miko hollered back. "Better safe than sorry."

The woman sighed and shook her head. "Sorry about him."

I grinned. "Don't be. He's hilarious."

The woman walked calmly down the steps. "I'm Georgie. Lisha told us you were coming. Miko is my dad. He's an OG."

Miko huffed around the house. "I'm a Kook. Just say it."

My mouth dropped open. "You're original? I mean, you lived here when Goliath came?"

He nodded, an amused look on his lined face. "You better believe it. My family hunkered down when the storm came, because that's what we always did. It was too annoying to evacuate; the roads were always jammed. And we had a tradition of shooting off fireworks when the eye came. But then the eye never left, and neither did the storm. And climate change my butt, but that just doesn't happen. So someone captured the dang thing."

Georgie smiled and linked her arm through Miko's. "Okay, Pops, let's get them inside and you can tell your whole story. I think they want to get out of the stench."

Miko scowled. "What stench? The sweet aroma of money, you mean?"

Dad laughed. "I told you."

Miko grinned at Dad. "Ah, here's a smart guy. Lisha was right; ya'll are going to make a real difference to the team. I think we're finally going to get somewhere with shutting down this abomination."

I stepped forward. "Lisha said you'd introduce us to the team. And you'd tell us what your plan is so far. Because we have no idea how to shut this down."

A grim look came across Georgie's face. "Well, we've had a plan for years. But what we haven't had is the manpower to carry it out."

I nodded. "That's what Lisha said. And we have willing bodies. But she didn't go into any details about what we have to do."

Miko and Georgie held a conversation with their eyes and seemed to decide that we passed some kind of test.

"Welp, come on in. I can't offer you sweet tea because we ran out of tea bags years ago. But I can offer you something better than that." Miko turned and began his ascent up the rickety-looking steps.

"Please let it be soda," Luca said. "I'm dying for soda."

Miko stopped and looked over his shoulder. "You and me too, boy. But I haven't had a lick of that stuff for forty-five years. Nope, all I can offer you is the secrets of the eye."

CHAPTER 17

I FELT INSTANT RELIEF as I entered the farmhouse, as if I had been smothered by a thick, cloying blanket of chicken stench, and finally took a breath of fresh air.

Miko hiked up his pant legs and plopped into a recliner that looked as ancient as he was. "Notice anything about the smell? How completely it covers the delightful aroma of the chickens?"

Luca and Dad looked lost, but I nodded. "I can breathe again."

Georgie grinned. "Amazing, right? My mom developed that air freshener, and now they use it all over the City."

I took a big whiff, and it hit me. "Oh, that's the smell of the Med Center. Very calming."

She gestured to some worn-looking couches. "Yeah, the med centers are my best customers."

Miko turned on an intense stare. "But do you see what I'm getting at?"

I looked to Georgie, at a complete loss. "It's a great smell. Like lavender and vanilla? But not overpowering at all."

She gave a small smile. "Dad is terrible at giving hints. He's trying to point out that the smell of the chickens has been eliminated."

Luca settled onto the couch and leaned his head back. "That's good, right?"

Miko snorted. "Well, it's good for business. But if my daughter wasn't so good at her job, maybe we wouldn't be in this pickle."

Georgie threw up her hands. "Dad, come on. We've been over this a thousand times. My air freshener is not keeping everyone in the dark. It's just making life better."

I was so confused. "You want things to smell like chickens?"

Miko's face turned red. "I want things to smell like they smell. And the smell of Goliath would drive people away from here faster than a hen pecking at a kernel of corn."

"And since they didn't seem to care for the first thirty years, what makes you think they'll care now?" Georgie asked. "You never have a good answer to that question."

Things became silent and tense as Georgie and Miko stared each other down.

Dad cleared his throat. "Ah, is this a bad time to ask what Goliath smells like?"

Miko's face darkened. "Death. Stench. It smells like rotten eggs from the bacteria in the low-lying water that's been stirred up, and like decay from the fungus breaking down rotting wood. Instead, they blanket the entire City with my Georgie's tropical scents, so no one knows. No one can smell the blight of Goliath anymore, so they don't care about doing what we can to get rid of it."

Luca leaned forward. "Would it really make a difference?"

"Yes!" Miko slapped his leg. "People are too comfortable here. If the storm bothered them the way that it should, they'd be more willing to help us shut it down."

Georgie sat on her dad's arm rest. "And I think the smell isn't enough. The Renwicks have done a great job indoctrinating everyone to believe that the outside world wants to come in and steal all the things we have that make our lives so good. We have to get them to care about more than just themselves."

I studied Georgie's face. "I mean, that makes sense to me, but I'm from the outside. Like, the med tech here could change so many lives. But even I understand that no one here would care about that, because they know nothing of the outside world. I mean, why do *you* care? You were born here, right?"

Georgie nodded. "But I grew up hearing stories from Pops about what the outside was like. And here's what you have to know about most of us who were born in here; we want the chance to make our choices. To explore, to meet other people, to decide what we want to do with the rest of our lives. We've never been given the choice. I just think that people should be able to choose to live in this kind of isolation."

Miko grunted. "And then there's the whole thing about the population being drugged. I can tell you know about that. You have the shadows under your eyes of people who didn't sleep well because of those confounded rockets. Which means you didn't take your medicine last night."

Luca lifted his head off of the couch. "Now that we've heard the rockets, can we take the good stuff tonight?"

Georgie shook her head. "I really don't recommend it. It's better for you to get used to not taking them now. You've only been on them, what, two weeks? It'll be an easier detox if you go cold turkey. You'll sleep better, now that you're not so close to the site."

"Do you know what they're launching?" I asked. "Are they testing a way to get up and over the storm?"

Georgie and Miko glanced at each other. "It's a pretty locked-down facility, but one of our team members has the full scoop. They'll give you a report when we meet tonight."

A shot of adrenaline coursed through my veins. "We get to meet them tonight?"

Georgie grinned. "Yeah. And we have a surprise for you, too. But first, I'm sure you want a nap. Coming off the sleeping tabs is rough, even with the energy tabs. A nap will take the edge off."

I must not have been able to keep the disappointment off of my face, because Georgie gave me a sympathetic smile. "Trust me, you'll want to be rested for tonight. This meeting is going to go late, because we're finally going to make a solid action plan, and that might take a while."

Miko pulled on the side lever of his recliner to bring up the foot rest. "Y'all can do what you want, but I'm going to nap until lunch. Sound good, Georgie?"

She patted him on the leg. "Sure thing, Dad. I'll wake you when lunch is ready. You three, come with me. We've got beds upstairs for each of you."

Luca seemed to have already fallen asleep, and I felt bad for waking him, but I thought he might be more comfortable upstairs. Georgie pointed out a room with two twin beds for Dad and Luca, then took me down the hall to a beautiful corner room that overlooked the farm.

"Is this your room?"

She nodded. "Yeah. I grew up here."

I turned, surprised. "You didn't get married?"

Tears filled her eyes. "No, I wasn't chosen for that."

"Chosen?"

"The Renwicks choose who gets to go into the marriage pool. Well, their team does. Since our society is a contained society, they keep a close eye on the genetics, but also need to make sure we will not outgrow our resources. So we get evaluated when we turn eighteen, and then we're assigned. Either we're in the marriage pool and get jobs closer to the center of the City so we can meet a spouse, or we're not, and we're assigned to jobs on the outskirts of town."

My mouth dropped open. "And everyone accepts this?"

Georgie shrugged. "I guess to be fair, more people get put into the marriage pool than don't. So majority rules, and all that."

My heart broke for her. She was a pretty lady. I'm not sure why she would have gotten the short end of the stick.

She smiled. "I've made peace with it. I've gotten to live with Pops, and I was here when Mom passed away. If you're in the marriage pool, you can't leave your part of the City until you're married, so I know kids who have missed out on things with their parents."

I sank down onto the bed, still full of questions but so tired. "How did your mom die?" I covered my mouth with my hand. "I'm sorry. That's probably rude."

She shook her head. "No, it's not. She died of Huntington's disease."

"And the med center couldn't help?"

She gave a sad smile. "Mom refused to go. She didn't like how the tech was developed, and she refused to be a guinea pig."

Things clicked into place. "Do you have the gene?"

Georgie shrugged. "I didn't want to be tested. And even though they never said, I'm sure it's why I wasn't picked for the marriage pool."

I shook my head in disgust. "I can't believe that someone gets to tell you whether or not you can find love and get married."

She sighed. "I know. But I really do love my life, so it worked out. But I just think that everyone should have options, and living in Goliath means we have to live by other people's rules."

"Rules you probably don't even get to vote on."

She gave a little laugh. "Pops always told me about voting. It sounds so foreign, an idea that everyone gets to chime in on things. Part of me understands how chaotic that could be, so I get why our little City got rid of that the first chance they got. But enough of that." She backed away toward the door. "Get some sleep. I'll wake you up for lunch."

I laid my head back on a decorative pillow and almost instantly fell into a deep sleep. It was the kind of sleep that made feel I had slept for hours when I woke up, but it couldn't have been that long, because the first thing I smelled was fried chicken. It took me a few minutes to pinpoint the smell, because it had been weeks since I had had meat, but that smell was unmistakable. I jumped out of bed, worried that I had missed lunch, and hurried down the stairs.

I rushed into the kitchen, ready to give Dad and Luca an epic lecture about not waking me for fried chicken. But then I froze.

Adele Renwick stood next to Georgie, handing her a plate for the chicken.

I stood still and tried to decide if I had time to sneak out and find Dad and Luca so we could leave. But she turned and smiled.

"Hi, Ashlyn."

My heart raced like I had been caught doing something naughty. But I tried to remind myself that Adele gave us permission to go on this trip. And she even knew we were coming here, thanks to Lisha's broadcast on the surveillance at the Mayor's Mansion. The chicken farm was part of the tour, and I had no reason to be ashamed.

"Oh, um, hi, Adele. What are you doing here?" I smoothed back my messy nap hair and wanted to kick myself for sounding so stilted and awkward.

She grinned. "I never miss fried chicken day."

It took everything in me to keep my eyes from rolling. Of *course*, the person who imposed a vegetarian diet on the entire society under her thumb would take every advantage to not do what her subjects were required to do.

I pasted a smile on my face. "I could have sworn I smelled fried chicken, but then thought maybe I was just dreaming, since no one eats meat around here."

Georgie grinned at Adele. "That's the biggest perk at working at the chicken farm. We supply eggs for the City, so we get to eat the birds that no longer lay."

This chicken farm was growing on me. I tried to discreetly swallow the insane amount of saliva that had filled my mouth. "That's a good perk. Adele, can I get a transfer out here?"

She let out a ringing laugh that grated on my nerves. "If only job assignments were that easy."

I widened my eyes. "I mean, it is if you're the one in charge, right?"

She kept her smile, but narrowed her eyes a bit. "Well, you seem to understand the scope of my power, don't you?"

Georgie looked back and forth between us, a confused look on her face. "What's going on here?"

We were so close to getting Goliath shut down. I didn't want to do anything that would jeopardize our plans or the team, so I knew this was the perfect time to keep my mouth shut and play nice. "Nothing. I'm still trying to figure out how this City works. Sorry if I sound rude."

Adele pressed her lips together into a tight grin. "No worries at all. I prefer it when people direct all questions to me."

I bet she did. What better way to control the narrative?

She turned to the fridge and opened it like she had been living in this house her whole life. "Georgie, did you tell Ashlyn how we grew up together?"

I should be used to shocking things by now, but that still took me by surprise. "What? How? I mean, wouldn't you have grown up near City Hall, while Georgie lived way out here?"

Both Georgie and Adele cracked up over this. "See? It doesn't take long for people to think that we're a thousand miles away rather than ten miles outside of the City," Georgie said. She turned to me and grinned. "Adele's my cousin."

My mouth dropped open. "What?"

Adele laughed. "Our moms were sisters."

This did not make sense. How could Georgie and Miko be in the rogue group looking to shut down Goliath when they were related to the Renwicks?

Adele pulled a giant bowl of potato salad out of the fridge as Georgie took the last few pieces of chicken out of the pan of oil on the stove. Georgie handed me the plate of chicken. "Take this into the dining room, then tell your dad and everyone that lunch is ready."

I took the plate, barely able to stop myself from grabbing a piece and shoving it in my mouth as I walked. "Everyone?"

Adele grinned. "You'll see."

I sighed and hurried to put the chicken on the table. I stopped and stared for a second when I saw the enormous dining room table was set for twelve. The chatter of a group of people in the living room hit my ears. My heart rate picked up. Were we going to meet the rest of the team? With Adele in the house?

"Dad!" I yelled. "Lunch is ready!"

The noise of the group moved closer, and someone jumped into the room.

"Surprise!"

I almost dropped the chicken. "Jack?"

Jack grinned as Miri, Ginger, Silas, Hugh, and Cyra poured in behind him. "Happy graduation!"

I set down the plate and gave Dad a scowl as he and Luca followed the group in. "Dad. I said I did *not* want a stupid party."

Dad grinned. "No, you said you didn't want a stupid party with tofu hot dogs. This is fried chicken."

Jack hooted and plopped down in a chair.

I rolled my eyes. "You know what I meant."

Dad came over and put his arm around me. "Yeah, I do. And I didn't do this at all. I mean, I didn't set this up."

I raised an eyebrow. "Then who did?"

Adele stepped into the room with Georgie. "I did. I brought your friends here, because I wanted to make up for that other graduation present I gave you. Plus, Georgie said it was time for the team meeting. They were all hard at work at their jobs, but I have a little pull to get people out of work." She let out that annoying peel of laughter and winked at Miri. "I even got Miri from Weather Production, even though I could almost promise I assigned her to City Hall."

The group became silent as we all stared at Adele. My stomach sank. Did she know what we were planning to do? Luca stepped close to me, as if he were getting ready to fend off an attack.

Georgie glanced around the room. "You can relax, everyone. Adele's with us. She's on our side."

Miri folded her arms. "What side is that?"

Adele spread her hands out and smiled what looked like an actual smile this time. "Just call me Head Kook."

CHAPTER 18

NOT EVEN THE STEAMING plate of fried chicken made anyone move. It was like no one knew what to believe.

Miri broke the silence. "What are you talking about?"

I looked from Dad, to Luca, to Georgie. We hadn't even had a chance to talk with everyone yet about what we had seen and learned. Maybe this thing with Adele was a test, a trick to get us to spill information about the plans to stop Goliath.

Remorse crossed Georgie's face. "I'm sorry. I guess I should have told you about Adele."

I scowled. "You are aware she trapped us in here, right? She's an accessory to kidnapping?"

Adele shook her head. "No, that's not what's happening. Look, there are some things I have had to do because of my position as mayor, like working with USHA. But I've been working for a long time on a way to shut this down."

I rubbed my forehead, and my stomach growled. I needed food in order to process this.

"Now *this* is a smell you should develop for your line, Georgie!" Miko entered the dining room, tugging on his overalls. "More of the City should enjoy the fine aroma of a fried chicken. Ooo, Delly, when did you get here?"

Adele walked over and gave him an affectionate hug. "Hi, Uncle Miko."

Miko glanced around the room. "What're we all doing just standing there staring at the food? Y'all can eat."

They all looked at me. I sighed. "Then let's eat, I guess."

Everyone sat down, with the Storm Breakers on one end of the table, and Georgie, Miko, and Adele on the other. We were silent as we passed around the food.

Adele cleared her throat. "I know I owe you all an explanation, so just hear me out. My grandpa was the one who created the technology to capture and sustain the hurricane. Once he did that, his team was able to figure out how to manipulate the weather currents into on-demand tornados. Grandpa was a genius, and he was restless. Once they were confident they could sustain Goliath, he turned his focus to medical advances. He convinced the people who were caught in the eye with him that they were on their own and had to figure out how to take care of their own medical needs. He didn't explain to them what kind of experimentation would take place, but people could overlook the failed experiments and fatalities because of the good that happened. I mean, Miri, your spinal injury was healed, and you've experienced what the refreshers can do, right, Ashlyn?"

I narrowed my eyes and finished chewing my chicken. "Yeah. But does that make it okay?"

Adele rubbed her neck. "No, of course not. I'm sorry. I'm not explaining myself very well. Let me go back. When Grandpa caught the storm, no one in the eye knew what to do. But Grandpa did, so they looked to him, and agreed with everything he said. So when he said that democracy had failed the United States, and that it was best to pass on leadership, they agreed. When he said that experimentation was necessary for our medical advances, they agreed. When he said that everyone outside the storm would want to raid us and take what we had, they all agreed that Goliath was a blessing and should be protected. And when he said that every part of people's lives, from where they work to whom they marry, should be guided by people who understood what was best for our limited resources, they agreed. But of course, it wasn't right. They traded their freedom for safety and comfort, only they didn't realize that's what they were doing."

For the first time, Silas spoke. "But you're at the top of the food chain in here. Why should we trust you want to take down the storm?"

Adele's eyes glistened. "Georgie was my best friend growing up. And my mom and her mom were the best sisters. It hurt us all when Aunt Molly died. It hurt Mom so much that she shut herself away at the northern mansion. She's been there ever since. The worst part about being at the top is having to pretend all the atrocities are justified. My dad and grandpa have been training me since I was a girl to be the next mayor, but I have never been able to get past the idea that people weren't allowed to choose. I mean, look at Georgie. She's the best, and she wasn't allowed to marry, just in case she had the Huntington's disease gene. I even fought with them about it, but Dad said that if I didn't take over as mayor, then they'd have to find someone outside the family."

Miko broke in. "And only the mayor has access to the things we need to stop the storm. Adele had to be mayor."

We had all been eating during this sob story. How on earth could we believe her?

Adele leaned forward. "I sent you on this 'tour' at this time, because that's when the launches were scheduled. I sent you to the southern mansion because you'd be close enough to witness them. I'm the one who gives Lisha the right iron tabs, the ones without the sleeping agent. I made sure that Lisha sent you here, because we're going to have a team meeting today. And I brought your whole team, because I knew you would all want to be a part of this."

Luca held a steady, intense gaze on Adele. "Tell us about the launches."

Adele swallowed and nodded. "Grandpa wanted to capture Goliath to create this zone where he could work freely, but he also knew that he'd have to have the ability to leave to connect with suppliers outside the eye. You all know first hand how slow it is to move through Goliath. He enlisted the help of some of his friends in NASA, and they agreed to move operations to the old Orlando International Airport. Long story short, they've been working on shuttles that launch up and over Goliath to Buckley Space Force base in Colorado."

Dad set his mouth. "So, last night someone left the eye?"

Adele nodded. "Grandpa doesn't go much anymore, but he has his staff go for him. They bring back whatever he needs."

I wiped my mouth on a napkin and leaned back. "I think we can appreciate all the information. But there's one big piece to this puzzle missing, and that's your involvement with USHA. You know that USHA threatened my family, right? Matteo? The one you have sitting pretty in the Mayor's Mansion near City Hall?"

Adele nodded. "Yeah, and I'm so sorry about that. USHA was part of the plan all along. They were part of Grandpa's team back when this all started."

Ginger raised an eyebrow. "USHA wasn't formed until five years after the hurricane landed."

"Right, so that it wouldn't look suspicious. Plus, it took five years to truly stabilize Goliath, and so they could get control to allow in supplies."

Things clicked into place why Colorado Springs, Colorado was chosen as the headquarters for USHA. I wonder how many times Ashton had come to Colorado without us knowing it. The despotism of this place ruined my appetite for the fried chicken.

Miko grunted. "So many people died in those first five years because of the lack of supplies. It's why they were so thankful when Ashton finally gave them what they needed. Only a few people asked questions about where the supplies came from, and, ironically, those were the people who didn't make it through the medical experimentation process."

Silas leaned forward. "Of course, we all know this is bad. What we don't understand is why *you*, Adele, are willing to help us take it down."

"I guess the best way to say it is, I don't want to be like my dad. He enjoyed being in charge and calling the shots. He didn't care who got hurt in the process. But I just don't think that's right. Uncle Miko showed me that after Aunt Molly died, and once I realized what they were kept Georgie from the marriage pool just because she *might* have the Huntington's gene, I realized I didn't want to be a part of it anymore. I can't tell you how many people have looked at me in disappointment when I've handed out their job assignments, or when they find out they haven't been selected for the marriage pool. And really, it's for no reason other than control."

"So why don't you just change things in here?" Miri asked. "You're the mayor. You could change how the society is run without shutting down Goliath."

Frustration filled her eyes. "We're *all* trapped here. Me included. And I didn't ask to be. None of us did. Shutting down Goliath is the only way to set everyone free."

Jack started a slow clap and stood up. "Now *that's* American."

Cyra rolled her eyes and tugged him back down. He grinned and shoved a bite of potato salad into his mouth.

I glanced around the table. Silas and Ginger seemed to have a conversation with their eyes. Miri watched Adele with narrowed eyes. Luca had finished his food and had his arm stretched across the back of my chair. He raised one eyebrow when I made eye contact with him.

I pushed away my plate. "Ah, well, thank you for that presentation. And I don't want to be rude, but I think we should have time to talk. In private. I mean, I feel like you owe us that much, since you imprisoned us and all."

Adele gave a wry smile. "For what it's worth, it wasn't my idea. Chip was the author of that. But you're right, I *am* the one who allowed the increase in Goliath's power. It wasn't time to tip my hand just then. Anyway, sure. I understand. I'll, uh, go help Uncle Miko and Georgie with the chicken chores." She looked at Dad. "Jonah?"

Dad pressed his lips together and gave a nod. Relief covered Adele's face as she left the room with Georgie.

Miko stood up. "Y'all can trust her. I would never have brought her into the team if you couldn't. I know y'all think your cause is important, but we're the ones who have been fighting since Goliath landed. We would never bring anyone in who might hurt that. And that goes for you all, too. Shutting down this confounded storm is my life's work. I welcome anyone who wants to help, and I promise I will stop anyone who tries to stop us." With that, Miko shuffled out of the room, hollering out orders to Adele and Georgie. The back door of the kitchen banged shut, and their footsteps faded away.

I turned to Dad. "Why did she look at you like that?"

Dad sighed and rubbed the back of his neck. "I, ah, knew about Adele."

"Knew what?"

He wouldn't meet my eyes. "That she wanted to shut down the storm."

The room was silent as we all stared at him. My mind was blank. Finally, a question popped out. "Why didn't you tell us?"

Dad gave a little laugh and shook his head. "You're going to hate this, but I wanted to protect you. There are so many people in here who wouldn't hesitate to hurt you guys if they thought you were going to do something to Goliath. And honestly, you wouldn't be missed by anyone. Adele has had to keep things hidden so her dad and grandpa wouldn't find out, and I promised I would let her take the lead on when to let you all in on this."

I closed my eyes and rubbed my temples. "Dad. Please, no more secrets. Is there anything else you need to tell us?"

"Just that I promise I didn't know anything about the launches. Adele didn't tell me much either, for plausible deniability. I agreed to that, because I trust her."

Hugh folded his arms. "What launches are you talking about?"

Dad, Luca, and I interrupted each other for the next ten minutes, telling them everything we had seen and experienced on our trip. I hated to admit it, but everything we saw lined up with what Adele said.

Miri pursed her lips. "I still don't see what Adele will get out of this. I mean, this City is benefiting from Goliath. Why would anyone give that up?"

"For freedom!" Jack shouted. His face turned sheepish when none of us laughed.

I sighed. "Lisha and Lev said that in order to shut down the storm, they needed to shut down the six perimeter stations *and* Weather Production at the same time. That's seven different teams working together. They said that there are only ten people on their team right now, which I guess isn't enough. It sounds like more than one person needs to be in a place at a time."

Ginger nodded. "And Adele is probably the only one who can get into Weather Production."

I leaned back in my chair. This all sounded too good to be true.

Hugh leaned forward. "Here's what I think. Adele is legit. I mean, she has no reason to string us along on something like this. She could have just shut us away, made us work those boring jobs and sleep like the dead at night for the rest of our lives. I bet she had to keep up appearances to prove to Chip she was successful at subduing us. But I imagine you asking for that tour was just the opening she needed to show us what is actually going on here."

I had to hold back my surprise at two things. First, that Hugh talked that much. Second, that everything he said made sense.

Dad nodded. "It's more Ashton and Geno that she's had to convince. They may not be the mayor, but they still pull all the strings in this City. And they have eyes everywhere."

I snorted. "And bugs, apparently."

Silas pursed his lips. "So, do we tell them we're in?"

Luca gave a little growl. "I don't like that they're the ones calling the shots. I wish it was our plan."

Silas gave Luca a sad smile. "You sound just like your dad. He always had a hard time trusting a plan that wasn't his, or that he wasn't fully in control of."

I gave a little laugh. Was it really only two months ago that Tyler was giving me a hard time for being the lead on our raid of USHA? I laced my fingers through Luca's. "It'll be okay. We don't have any other option. If this is the chance we have, then we might as well, right?"

Jack wiggled in excitement. "Yeah, what would you rather do? Go back to those boring, dumb jobs that Adele gave us?"

Luca sighed. "No. You're right. We might as well."

"Good!" Miko stomped into the room, causing us all to jump.

I scowled. "Were you listening in?"

Miko chortled. "Of course I was. I told you, I welcome help, but will not put up with anyone who stands in our way.

I had to know if you all needed to be locked in the chicken coop for the duration of this mission."

I shuddered. I may have had a hard time trusting Adele, but there is no doubt Miko would do something like that.

For the first time since I met him, Miko's face became serious. "You all don't know how glad I am that you came through that storm. We've needed extra hands for years, and I was starting to worry that I might meet my maker before we could ever get it done. I look spry, but I'm reaching the end of my limit, and so is half of the team. We need energetic, quick people for this task." His voice became choked up. "It's going to happen."

I took a deep breath and allowed the flicker of hope to spring to life inside my chest. I wondered how long it would have taken us to figure out we needed to hit seven targets at once. Probably years. The rest of the team broke into chatter, speculating on how the mission was going to go down. Luca let go of my hand and turned to Miri, and for the first time, it didn't bother me. I was too excited to worry about Luca and Miri anymore.

I looked at Dad. "We're going home, Dad. For real."

Dad smiled a smile that didn't quite reach his eyes. "Yeah, I guess so. Sorry, it's just so hard to believe. I, uh, thought that I'd live the rest of my days here."

"And I thought I'd never see you again. And Mella and Trig and everyone thinks you're dead. But here we all are, wrong about everything."

Dad laughed and pulled me into a side hug. "Yeah, I guess I can admit when I'm wrong, too."

Adele poked her head into the room. "Is it safe to come back?"

Miko waved her in. "Coast is clear! Or it will be, as soon as we get this dang show on the road. They're in, and they're ready, Delly."

She smiled and looked relieved. "Oh, good. Then let's plan this thing. Because this has to go down tomorrow night."

Chapter 19

I took a deep breath in through my nose. The smell of chickens wasn't quite so strong on this side of the pond. Georgie and Miko must have been aware of that, because the bench beneath the large magnolia tree looked well used.

Luca tugged on my hand, and we sat together. I tried to suppress my smile when he sat very close to me, rather than taking advantage of the space on the bench.

"So?" he asked as he put his arm across the back of the bench.

I snuggled in. "I mean, it's the only plan we've got."

Adele and Miko had spent the last hour going over the basics of the plan to take out Goliath. The rest of the team would show up later that night for final assignments. There would be seven teams of two. Six teams would go inside the pillars that housed the lasers that supported the perimeter of the storm and shut them down. One team would enter Weather Production and hit the kill switch.

According to Adele, all these things needed to happen at the exact same time, and Goliath would simply dissolve away. If one station missed their timing, the storm would become unstable, and they would lose the ability to control its path. The City would be at risk, and so would the entire eastern seaboard of the United States, since Goliath could take a turn up the coast.

Luca sighed and rubbed my shoulder with his thumb. "I hate that we have to trust Adele's word."

I rested my hand on Luca's leg. "Hugh is right. She is the one with the power to keep us sedated or locked away. And yes, she seems to be the one orchestrating everything, but she has the authority to do it. That's what we needed; an in."

We were silent for a few minutes, watching the peaceful pond. I still hadn't gotten used to the incredible juxtaposition of this place. This farm was idyllic, with giant palms, fronds, and ferns all over, and ducks swimming lazily around the lily pads. A gentle breeze blew away the smell of the hundreds of chickens in their free range pen on the other side of the property. And towering in the distance were the angry, swirling clouds of Goliath.

Luca shifted beside me. "So. When we shut down the storm, then what?"

I turned to him. "We go home. Right?"

He looked unsure. "Yeah, but what happens when we get home? I mean, you know, with everything."

"What are you talking about?"

He sighed, removed his arm, and leaned forward, staring at the pond. "I mean you had real plans for what would happen after you graduated high school. And it sounds like Mason is still in the picture. And I've spent my whole life focused on the Storm Chasers with my dad. But my dad is gone. And if this works, the Storm Chasers will dissolve, too. I mean, there won't be a storm to chase anymore, will there? So, are you just going to go back to your life?"

My heart turned over, and I looped my arm through his. "Hey," I said. I waited for him to look at me. "Mason is *not* in the picture. I have no desire to reconnect with him or anything."

A grin appeared. "Really?"

I pulled his face to mine and kissed him. He seemed hesitant at first, but then responded in the way I was hoping. I tried to keep my wits about me and pulled away after a few minutes.

I laughed at his dopey smile. "You see?"

Luca sighed and put his arm across the bench again, and I settled in next to him. "Yeah, I see. But Booker, what am I going to do? I've never made any plans beyond the Storm Chasers."

"One day at a time, Denzio." I almost laughed. Two months ago, I never would have been so relaxed about the future. I had everything planned out, and I loved it. I was going to Eckman University with Mason, and we'd get married, and live our lives working jobs and raising a family. But then Chip entered the picture and forced me on this journey to find Dad. And not only did I find him, but we found a way to shut down the storm. So everything had changed.

"I'll have to get an actual job, I guess."

That made me laugh. "Well, you've shown a real knack for maintenance."

He groaned. "No way. I never want to see another mop again."

I snuggled in next to him. "Hey, I have no idea what I'm going to do, either. I mean, I'm not sure if college is what I want anymore. So I'm in the same boat."

"Attention. There will be people in your vicinity in twenty seconds. I repeat, you have twenty seconds to finish any PDA." Jack's voice came through the fronds behind us.

I rolled my eyes. "We're not doing anything."

Jack, Cyra, and Miri emerged through the bushes. Jack had a wicked grin on his face. "That's why I gave you the warning."

Cyra punched him in the arm. "Stop making this weird."

Miri folded her arms and plopped down on the other side of Luca. "So, are we doing this thing?" It didn't escape my notice that she didn't acknowledge anything Jack said or how Luca and I were sitting.

Luca leaned back and put his hands behind his head. "I guess we have to."

Cyra plopped right down on the pokey grass. "My parents would freak out if they knew I was part of this."

I studied her face. "So you had no idea that Adele wanted to shut down Goliath?"

She shook her head hard. "No. Way. I mean, to be fair, I've never spent *that* much time with her. She's the freakin' mayor. She's busy."

Miri grinned. "But isn't Pax your 'special friend?'"

Her cheeks turned bright pink, and she glanced at Jack. "Ugh, no. I mean, he's my friend, and he *wishes* he could be my special friend. But it's not like I ever hung out with him at the Mayor's Mansion. No one goes there except the Renwick family. Pax would always come to my house, or we'd hang at the park and stuff."

I didn't blame Cyra for not knowing about Adele. I only started paying attention to what my mom did when I realized how intertwined she was with Chip.

"And you don't think Pax knows at all?" I asked.

Cyra leaned back. "Nah. Pax doesn't really like his mom. He spends most of his time with his grandpa."

"Have you ever met him?"

"Nope. Like I said, no one goes to the Mayor's Mansion. It's, like, totally off-limits. Mom always made sure that I knew the Renwicks deserve their privacy. We're allowed to line up and shake their hands and stuff when they come out for public appearances, but no one would dare try to go to their home."

It was all so weirdly reminiscent of how the citizens of England treated their royalty. Clearly, Ashton Renwick patterned his utopian society after them.

"So, are we just going to sit around and let Adele tell us what team we're on?" Miri asked. I smiled. For the first time since Tyler died, the gruff, no-nonsense Miri seemed to be back.

I shrugged. "Do we have a choice?"

She leaned forward. "Yeah, we do. I'm getting real tired of sitting around, waiting for others to tell me what to do. And don't give me, 'they're the grown-ups' bit. We are, too. Well, not Jack and Cyra, but I'm over eighteen. I'm a legal adult."

Everyone stared at Miri in surprise. Jack and Cyra looked uncomfortable, and Luca looked perplexed.

"What's up with you, Day?" he asked.

"Nothing. Except I had a medical procedure done that I did not consent to, and I've been fed sleeping pills for the past two weeks, and I had no idea."

"Miri," I said. "That procedure saved your life."

She set her mouth. "Maybe. But what else did it do? I'm just saying they've altered us without our consent. I can't wait to get home to talk to a real doctor to find out what they've done."

And that was the problem with this secret society. How could anyone make informed choices about anything when the only people who had the full information were the Renwicks?

"What's your plan?" Luca asked. "Do you have a better option?"

Her eyes narrowed. "I just don't want to be split up."

My stomach twisted with guilt. I knew where this was coming from. She was still upset about being separated from Luca in the Turtles back in Traxler. The anger on her face when she got reassigned to the Turtle with Hugh, Ginger, and Jack rivaled Goliath's wrath. And then they got sucked up and tossed by that tornado.

There were going to be seven teams. There were nine of us Storm Breakers. Which meant that we could all be assigned to a different team, except for maybe two of us. But which two would be the lucky two? Of course, I wanted to stay with Luca. But Dad would probably insist that we stay together. I know Cyra and Jack wanted to be together, and Silas and Ginger would probably stay together for the same reason Miri had.

"Here's the thing," I said. "We *have* to be split up. There needs to be at least one of us on every single team. Because we are the only people I trust."

Miri shook her head. "No, dividing us is how they'll get full control over us. Splitting up would be so stupid."

My heart pounded. She was being so unreasonable right now. I clenched my fists. "I thought the whole point of the Storm Chasers was to stop the storm. This is the first, and probably only, real chance we have to do that. And now you're not willing to do what it takes? I want to go *home*. Chip is still calling the shots out there, and he has to be stopped. He thinks he has us trapped in here for ten years, so he won't be looking for us to make a move. The time is now. We have to do what it takes."

Luca put his hand on my leg. "Calm down, Booker. It's going to happen. We just have to hash out how." He looked at Miri. "Right?"

Miri folded her arms and slumped down. "I will not be on a team by myself. If that means the mission is off, fine. But I refuse to do something I know is stupid." She looked right at Luca. "Remember how sure you were that you needed to leave Silas? That's how sure I am about this. And remember how I trusted you and went along with you? Why can't you do that for me?"

I closed my eyes and tried to think. Of all the roadblocks we could come up against, I never dreamed that our group would be the one to shut this down. Obviously, there was one answer, and I was going to have to be the one to take one for the team.

I opened my eyes. "Okay, Miri. How about we tell them you and Luca have to stay together?"

Luca's head whipped toward me, surprise in his eyes. Then confusion. I could tell he wanted to protest, but I put my hand on his arm.

"It's the best plan," I said. "I'll be okay. And Miri needs you for this. It'll be fine."

Miri's face was tense as she watched Luca and me. Luca's eyes softened, and he turned back to Miri. "Would that work for you, Day?"

Her eyes filled with tears, and her face turned red in the classic way that happens when people try not to cry. "Yeah. That would work." Her face crumpled, and she buried her head in her hands. "Sorry. I just can't be separated from you again. I mean, I thought I was dead."

Jack leaned over and patted her on the leg. "We get it. You did almost die."

I shot him a dirty look. "Jack."

He shrugged. "Sorry. I just know what she means."

Compassion filled my chest. Jack had been on that Turtle, too. "Are *you* okay if you're on a team without one of us?"

He glanced at Cyra and straightened. "Yeah, I'm cool. I mean, I *didn't* almost die. So I'll be okay."

Luca gave him a brotherly pat on the arm. "Okay. We have our terms. Miri and I stay together. The rest of you split up. And I can think of one more condition that we should make a non-negotiable."

I tried to figure out what he was talking about by studying his face, but nothing came to mind.

Luca turned to me. "I think you should be the one to go into Weather Production with Adele."

I raised my eyebrows. "Why?"

"Because Ginger, Hugh, and Silas should be on the perimeter teams. Miri and I will be on a team together. And your dad has spent ten years under the City's influence, so I don't fully trust him yet. It has to be you."

I let out a laugh. "There's no way."

Luca shrugged. "It's our condition. If they won't let you on that team, none of us will do this. And if they would rather scrub the mission than let you on that team, then we know where they stand, which is they don't care if Goliath gets shut down or not."

A lump formed in my throat. "And what if that happens?"

Luca grinned. "Then we'll figure out how to do it on our own some other time. They told us what needs to be done."

A clanging sound rang out across the pond.

"What is that?" Jack asked. "A cowbell?"

I smiled. "Sounds like it. Well, let's go tell Adele how this is going to work. If she agrees, we can be sure that she's legit, don't you think?"

Luca stood up and nodded. He reached for my hand, and we followed Jack and Cyra back around the pond.

Miri hung back to walk with us, a meek look on her face. "Uh, thanks. Sorry that I freaked out on you like that."

Luca let go of my hand and wrapped his arm around Miri's shoulders. I wasn't even jealous. She needed a friend. She had stayed by Luca's side as Tyler died, and it was time to stand by her. I ran to her other side and looped my arm through hers.

"Whatever you need, Miri. Because we need your tenacity." I gave her a smile, and she smiled back.

"Let's go send Goliath back to the pit, then," she said.

CHAPTER 20

Apparently, there was one more reason why we needed one member from the Storm Breakers on each team. Everyone else was *old*. I mean, besides Georgie, Lisha, and Lev, no one else was under the age of seventy. Three men and a woman had come in with Lisha and Lev, looking like the excitement of what was happening might make them keel over. Their eyes were bright and clear, but their bodies looked like they had been through it. I had no idea how they would be able to help with any kind of mission.

The old woman chuckled when she saw our faces. "I know what you think. We just never trusted those refreshers, so this is what it looks like when you age naturally, my friends. The way God intended."

Georgie grinned and put her arm around the woman's shoulders. "This is Annette. She's pretty proud of her body."

Annette stood up as straight as her hunched back would allow her. "I earned every one of these years, living inside this infernal storm. No one is going to erase that."

Adele walked in and smiled at Annette. "We celebrate your right to choose how to live. That's the point of this, yes?"

She grunted and moved to sit on the couch.

We had crammed into Miko and Georgie's living room, us young people sitting on the floor. Yes, Dad, Silas, Ginger, and Hugh were considered some of the young people.

Adele stood in the doorway. "This is it, folks. The day we've been waiting for. We have to do this tomorrow night."

"Why?" Miri asked.

"Goliath is on a seven-day cycle. It draws energy from the harvesters on Sunday, then runs for a week. We need to hit the pillars when the energy at the pillars is at its lowest point, just before midnight on Saturday. Otherwise, the storm will be too self-sufficient, and we risk simply setting it free."

"Plus," Miko said. "That's when the pillars are safe to enter. I know, because I worked on the pillar crews back in my youth, before I settled down with my wife here with the chickens. The pillars have too much voltage at any other time, and any one of you could end up crispier than that chicken leg you ate earlier."

Hugh tapped his mouth. "I thought it was warmer here on Sundays. But we'd only been here two weeks, so I figured I just wasn't used to the tropics yet."

Miko leaned forward and grinned. "Y'all are smart. I knew the fresh blood is exactly what we needed."

Georgie rolled her eyes. "Don't be creepy, Dad. If we don't do it tomorrow, we have to wait another week. But we're all together now; getting the whole group together without drawing attention is difficult enough that I'm not sure we could do it again soon without someone asking questions."

Silas cleared his throat. "So, clearly you all have worked on this plan. How are we supposed to do this?"

Georgie stood up and pulled out a large roll of paper. Lisha grabbed one end, and they stretched it across the room.

"Whoa, is that a map?" Jack asked, looking bug-eyed.

Cyra rolled her eyes. "Of course it is, doofus."

Miri smirked. "In the real world, we don't use a lot of paper. To preserve the trees and all."

The City people looked baffled by this concept. Adele shrugged and moved on. "For the sake of our new friends, here are the locations of the pillars at each corner of the City. There are two pillars per station, and each need to be shut down simultaneously, or else we risk the storm moving."

Hugh leaned forward. "And how do we do that?"

Adele stepped aside as Lev stood up. "We need to send teams of two to each pillar. Inside, there is a kill switch at the base of the pillar and a kill switch at the top. They have to be pressed within five seconds of each other, or the lasers on top won't shut off. And no one could climb the ladder in five seconds to reach the one at the top."

Jack looked stricken. "Climb? How high?"

"About one hundred and forty feet. The pillars are ten stories high." Lev studied Jack. "Will that be a problem? Because we specifically need you to be one of the climbers."

Jack looked a little pale, but he shook his head. "No, I can do it."

Luca punched him in the arm. "We'll race. Loser buys the tacos when we get out of this dump."

One of the old men, Carson, sighed. "Tacos. I miss tacos. They don't have them in here."

Luca grinned. "The loser will buy you tacos, too."

Adele cleared her throat. "But before that can happen, the master code has to be entered in at Weather Production. That has to be done by two people at the exact same time. The pillars have to be shut down within two minutes of the codes at Weather Production."

The room was silent as we all contemplated this. It sounded simple enough, yet a lot of things needed to happen at a very specific time.

Dad cleared his throat. "Okay, so I'm guessing Adele is going to Weather Production. Does that mean you'll be directing all of this from there?"

A grim look came over her face. "Here's the kicker: we can't use communications of any kind. Radio chatter is monitored at all hours, and I can't shut that down without bringing attention to us. The last thing we need is someone showing up at the pillars."

"You mean you don't control security?" I asked.

Adele shifted. "I do, to a point. But Dad and Grandpa are still heavily involved. You still don't understand how loyal most citizens of the City are to the storm. It's been their whole life's purpose. Protect the storm."

Dad sighed. "Yeah, I get that. So, we synchronize watches?"

Our expressions must have shown something, because the Old Timers cracked up.

"Y'all should see the confusion," Carson gasped out. "I bet you've never even seen a watch."

Miri glared at him. "Why would we? Back home, there are screens everywhere. Watches are redundant."

Annette tsked. "So, convenience has finally replaced elegance. I always made fun of my mom for saying that would happen one day. Are we sure we want to rejoin that world, boys?"

Carson grunted. "Heck, yes. I'll give up my watch and elegance for a taco."

Adele jumped in. "So this confirms that we need one City person and one Storm person per team. The City person will keep the time and handle the lower switch, while the Storm person will climb and hit the upper switch."

I glanced at Luca and Miri. It was exactly what we thought would happen. But Dad wasn't prepared for it.

"Can I count as a City person, because I know how to use a watch?" he asked. "I want Ashlyn on my team."

I shook my head. "No. I want to go to Weather Production."

Dad wore a familiar expression from my youth. It was the look of a parent who was putting their foot down. Usually he left that to Mom, except on the few occasions when he had to intervene in some dumb scheme my brothers had concocted.

"No, you're coming with me, and that's final."

The room grew silent and tense as everyone got caught in the showdown between me and Dad.

I folded my arms and lifted my chin. "It's our non-negotiable. We decided. I go to Weather Production, or this mission is a no-go."

His face turned red. "This is way too dangerous, and I don't want to be separated from you."

Adele leaned forward and put her hand on Dad's shoulder. "Jonah, she'll be safe with me. You know that."

He looked like he was about to argue, but he knew better than anyone that we didn't have time for that. His eyes filled with resignation. "Fine. But I don't like it."

Lev and Lisha exchanged glances, and Lisha squeezed Lev's hand and nodded. Lev raised his hand. "I'll go with you, Jonah. I'll even be the climber."

Dad sighed and nodded.

Miri cleared her throat. "And I'm with Luca."

Adele frowned. "I said one Storm person, one City person per team."

Miri stared at Adele in defiance. "I can learn to work a watch. It's also non-negotiable."

Miko threw his hands in the air. "Kids, this mission is more important than your drama. Enough with the non-negotiables."

Luca put his hands up to calm Miko down. "It's our last one, okay? Miri almost died the last time we got separated, so I don't think it's unreasonable."

Adele sighed. "Fine. Ashlyn is with me. Lev is with Jonah. Luca is with Miri. Then Silas and Carson, Ginger and Lisha, and Hugh and Georgie."

Jack's eyes brightened. "And me and Cyra?"

Adele shook her head. "No, you're with Annette."

"What?" Cyra exploded. "She's a million years old!"

Annette shook her finger at Cyra. "And a million years smarter than you, sweetheart. I can handle this if the young pup climbs."

Cyra clenched her fists. "What am I supposed to do, then?"

Dad and Adele exchanged glances.

"This is dangerous, and you're underage. Your parents would never forgive me," Dad said.

Cyra's face was purple with rage. "You can't just shut me out. I'm part of this team."

Adele gave her a compassionate look. "Jonah's right. It's for the best. I'm sorry."

"You could stay with me, Jonny, and Nate," Miko said, gesturing to the other old men. "We'll school you at cribbage while we wait for the good word of the mission's success."

Cyra huffed and stormed out of the room, then out of the house, slamming the door as she left. Miko shrugged at the other men. Jack jumped up to follow, but Silas stopped him.

"Let her go. We need to finish the plan."

Jack sighed and sat back down. "Okay, but you shouldn't underestimate her."

Adele chuckled. "Oh, trust me. I don't. Now, let's assign a pillar to each team. Tomorrow morning you'll head to a part of the City closest to your pillar, so you're ready to go at night. We'll just need reasons why you're in that part of the City. Your team needs to leave after ten p.m., to make sure everyone is asleep for the night. Any sooner could draw suspicion. You'll drive to the energy harvesting facility and pick up the maintenance humvee that will be safest to drive that close to Goliath's eyewall."

Annette cleared her throat. "This young man and I will take the southeast pillar. My niece lives in that part of town, and I can say I'm visiting her."

Lisha spoke. "Ginger and I will take the eastern pillar. It's an easy drive from the Mayor's Mansion."

Adele nodded. "Silas and Carson, you take the northeastern pillar. I'll tell Nash that I've sent you that way to get the maintenance reports from the energy harvester up that way. Hugh and Georgie, you take the southwest pillar. It's not too far from City Hall, and Georgie can say she's visiting me. Jonah and Lev can go for the western pillars, since that's near to Jonah's warehouse, and Luca and Miri can take the northwestern pillar. That's the pillar you drove by on the way in."

Luca cleared his throat. "Aren't there several pillars? How will we know which one to go to?"

Adele and Georgie unrolled another map. "The furthest pillar on the right-hand side has the switches. I'm not going to lie; it's the windiest out by those pillars. But that's because those were the first pillars built, and Grandpa built more at each station as he realized we were harvesting more power than expected, and could use that to strengthen Goliath and begin to experiment with tornado creation."

"Great," Luca muttered.

My heart skipped a beat, and I second guessed our plan about me being separated from Dad. I had been in those winds before, but never in the dark. What if he didn't make it? He had to survive this so that Mom and Trig and Mella and Penn could all see that he's alive.

"Ashlyn," Adele said. The way everyone was looking at me made me wonder how many times she had said my name. "It's going to be fine. The storm will be at its weakest, remember? Our humvees can handle that wind. Everyone can drive right up next to the pillar. No one has to walk far."

Dad gave me a small smile. "Now that I think about it, you going to Weather Production is a brilliant plan. I can do this, knowing you're no where close to those winds."

I put on a brave face. "For the record, I also can handle the wind. I came through the storm, didn't I?"

Annette leaned forward, her eyes shining. "When this is all over, can you tell me about what it was like? I've stared at those clouds every day for the past fifty years, and I've always wondered what it would be like to just walk out into Goliath."

I grinned and patted her hand. "Of course. Over tacos, right?"

She wrinkled her nose and recoiled. "No, thank you. Those never did agree with me. But I do miss hot dogs. Maybe we can find a good hot dog place."

I laughed. "My dad always grilled the best hot dogs. I bet he'll make one for you when this is done, right, Dad?"

Dad gave Annette a warm smile. "Of course, I will. A real one, not one of those tofu dogs we've been eating in here for years."

She gave a brisk nod. "So, what's next, then? Because I'll need to get my beauty sleep if I'm going to be fresh as my young man for our adventure tomorrow."

Adele smiled as Jack blushed. "We just have to go over the schematics of the switches, then you can head off to bed, Annette."

I stretched my neck and leaned forward to pay attention to everything Adele had to say. I was having a bit of FOMO since I wasn't on the pillar teams, but knowing what they would be doing helped me feel like I was a part of it. But even the FOMO couldn't stop the excitement from growing in my belly. We were so close.

CHAPTER 21

IF WE HADN'T SPENT so many nights crowded together in the shelters through Goliath, I might have felt awkward waking up in the crazy co-ed slumber party that took place in Georgie's living room. But we were used to it. The only difference was looking out the window to see sunshine, rather than the dark skies of a storm.

The Old Timers had taken the bedrooms in the farmhouse, so the rest of us Storm Chasers stretched out in the living room. Dad slept in the middle of the room, as if he was the boundary between the boys and the girls. A bittersweet smile crossed my face. Tyler would have done the same thing.

I let my gaze roam over the whole team, warm fuzzies filling my soul. Miri slept next to me, her face fierce even while she slept. Silas and Ginger slept near each other, but end to end with their feet touching. Hugh sacked out on the couch above Silas. Luca slept with his head buried under his blanket. Jack slept like a puppy, curled up in Miko's arm chair.

I felt bad for Jack. Cyra had taken off with Dad's golf cart, and I know he regretted not chasing after her when she stormed out. But his loyalty to the team was solid. When this was all over, I wanted to introduce him to Rosalie. He was younger than me and my friends back home, but he was way better than Zed, Rosalie's current crush. He and Rosalie would be a great match.

Dad stirred in his spot and opened his eyes. He gave me a sleepy smile, slowly sat up, and pointed at the door with a question in his eyes. I nodded and pushed off my blanket, then tiptoed out of the room and eased open the creaky back door. The scent of chicken was fainter on the back porch this morning, so I sat on the porch swing. Dad sat next to me, and for a few minutes, we sat in silence, staring at Goliath in the early morning light.

"I've stared at that storm for ten years now. And it still never ceases to amaze me."

I looped my arm through Dad's and rested my head on his shoulder. "It's awesome. I mean, I want to go home, but I'm a little sad to think it's going to be gone."

Dad nodded and pushed the swing back and forth. "It's been there my whole life. And yours. I can't imagine life without it."

I looked up at him. "But it's the right thing to do, right? I mean, it should never have been here like this."

He sighed. "Yes, it's the right thing. As soon as it's gone, people will know about the technology that created it. And that's the most important thing. No one should have that kind of power, at least not without oversight."

"So, we'll never see another hurricane again?"

"I don't know. If we can stop this unnatural one, we may see regular hurricanes again once the atmosphere returns to normal. Or maybe we can figure out how to use the technology to repel them from populated areas."

I sat up straight, my mouth open. "Whoa. That's really smart, Dad."

He chuckled. "Well, I'm a smart guy. I got my doctorate in climate studies and meteorology, you know. Back in my old life."

I shook my head. "I had no idea."

He laughed out loud and put his arm around my shoulders. "How did you think I got to be deputy director of USHA?"

I shrugged. "Who knows how adults get jobs?"

Dad kept his arm around me while still pushing us back and forth on the swing. "Well, in the real world, people find jobs they're interested in. They study and get the training they need to qualify, and then to advance in their field. Not like here, where a committee decides what you're going to do."

"And how do they pick what they want to study?"

Dad turned his head to look at me. "Well, what were you going to pick?"

I sighed and wrinkled my nose. "Accounting."

His eyebrows shot up. "Really?"

A bitter taste filled my mouth. "Yeah. Because I planned to set up an at home business to run while raising babies, since Mason was going to be a pastor."

Dad stopped rocking. "Whoa. You thought about marrying him?"

I swallowed hard. "I was young and stupid."

He squeezed me. "No. I mean, you were young, but not stupid. It's okay to dream and make plans."

I wiped the tear off of my cheek that sneaked its way out. I wasn't sad about Mason. I was embarrassed about how far

I had let my imagination take me with him. It had almost made me make actual life choices based on a fantasy. "Well, that's done. And now I don't know what's next."

Dad was quiet for a few minutes. "You have time, Mini Muffin."

I let out a soft laugh as a lump formed in my throat at his use of Mom's nickname for me. "Dad."

"Yeah?"

"Is turning off Goliath the right thing to do if it means our family is in danger?"

Dad's arm tightened as his muscles tensed up. "I choose to trust and believe that they'll be okay. We'll talk to authorities as soon as we can. If we tell a story of how they've been threatened, and then they're harmed, I think it will work in our favor. But, Honey, I knew Chip. I just can't believe that he would harm your mom. He really did love her. I have to believe that he was bluffing when he made his threats."

"I'll make sure they're okay."

We jumped at the sound of Adele's voice. I hadn't even heard her come outside. I tried to hide my surprise at her sleepy, unpolished appearance. It wasn't a look I had seen on her yet.

"How?" The question came out harsher than I intended. I wasn't trying to be rude, but I needed to know.

Adele walked over and leaned against the railing at the edge of the porch. "I have contacts at USHA that aren't Chip. People who have been in place for a long time, who have been ready in case Goliath was ever turned off."

This surprised me. "Are you kidding me? Why didn't they work with the Storm Chasers?"

Adele shrugged. "There was nothing they could do from there. The storm has always been controlled in here. But we can trust them. I'll contact them today to put out a watch on your family."

Dad's shoulders dropped as relief washed over his face. "Thank you, Adele."

She gave him a sad smile. "It's the least I can do. I know how much pain this storm has caused you. So many innocent lives. I'm doing what I can to make it right."

I stared at her. I couldn't help it. She was so different from when I first met her that I was having a hard time knowing who was real, Mayor Adele or this Adele?

Georgie stuck her head out of the back door. "Delly, breakfast is ready. You want to eat before you go?"

Adele checked her watch. "Yeah, if we're quick. I need to pull out in ten minutes. Jonah, you, Ashlyn, and Lev need to come with me since Cyra took your cart."

My heart pounded and fear threatened to take over. This was it. As soon as we left this house, our plan would begin.

Dad stood and entered the house with Adele. I wasn't hungry. I just wanted to talk to Luca. I jumped up to run inside just as the back door swung open.

Luca rushed out and grabbed me in a hug. "Adele said you were loading up to leave."

I nodded, my face buried in his chest. I wanted to kiss him, but I hadn't brushed my teeth since waking up, and that's not how I wanted our last kiss to go.

He laid his head on mine. "This is going to work, Booker."

"But will we survive?"

He pushed me back and looked into my eyes. "Heck, yeah, we will. I promise to. Do you?"

The confidence in his face siphoned some of the fear away. I nodded. "I promise."

He grinned, and I almost kissed him. But then I stepped back, putting space between us. His grin disappeared into confusion.

I held my hand up in front of my mouth. "I haven't brushed my teeth."

He let out a shout of laughter and pulled me close into a gentle hug again. "Fine. But make sure you brush your teeth after the mission, okay? Like, as soon as the storm fizzles."

My cheeks grew warm, and I nodded. "You, too, Denzio."

Dad, Lev, and Adele came out of the house. I intertwined my fingers with Luca's one more time, and he kissed the back of my hand.

"Okay, Romeo, let her go," Dad said. "Ash, it's time to go. Is your stuff ready?"

I nodded. "I just need to grab my bag." I reluctantly let go of Luca and ran into the house to grab my pack. I poked my head in the dining room where the rest of the team was eating.

"Good luck, guys," I said.

Jack grinned and waved, his mouth full of food. Silas and Hugh both nodded.

Ginger smiled. "We'll see you after."

Miri jumped up from the table and nodded toward the front door. I waved at everyone a final time, then followed her.

"Um, I'm sorry for making it so Luca had to come with me," she said in a soft voice. "It was a real baby move. But I need to stay with him."

My heart turned over at the sight of her red cheeks. I hadn't seen embarrassment on her before. "Don't be. It makes total sense. And honestly, this is best. I have to go to Weather Production, and it's not like anyone else could have come with me. Besides, I feel better knowing you and Luca are together. You can handle anything."

She gave me one of her classic, defiant grins. "Yeah, I can. We're gonna kick that pillar's butt. Good luck, Booker." She nodded once, then went back to the dining room.

I took a deep breath and headed outside, trying to ignore the dread that threatened to creep up my throat. I didn't know why I was reacting this way. We had done plenty of dangerous things since leaving Denver. In theory, this was the safest plan we had the whole time. But I couldn't rationalize the doom away.

Dad, Lev, and Adele were sitting in the golf cart, waiting. Luca stood at the bottom of the porch, an encouraging smile on his face.

"This is it, Booker. See you tomorrow." He leaned over and kissed my cheek. I gave him a smile, and then ran to the cart and jumped next to Dad in the backseat.

Adele twisted around from the driver's seat, a twinkle in her in eye. "Aw, you guys are so cute."

Dad grunted. "I wouldn't say cute."

My cheeks grew warm, but I kept my eyes on Luca as Adele pulled away from the farm.

It was weird to hear Lev and Adele chatter on the way back to City Hall. They were going over the logistics of how Goliath would shut down, and where we were all supposed to meet when it was over. If I closed my eyes, I could picture

Hugh and Ginger having the same conversation. It was almost like Adele was one of the Storm Chasers.

Adele pulled over just before we entered the main section of town. She turned to us with a solemn look on her face.

"Lev, I'll need you to drive from here to City Hall. It's time for me to be mayor again. It'll make more sense to people if I'm driven rather than the one driving."

Lev nodded and hopped out so Adele could slide over. I rolled my eyes.

Dad patted my leg. "We just have to keep up the optics for a few more hours, Ash. You can do it."

Adele gave me an embarrassed smile. "Remember, this is what people expect. It's important to do what they expect so that we can do the next part under the radar."

I had never been out in the City during the morning rush hour, so I had never seen so many people commuting to their jobs. They were delighted to see Adele driving among them. So many people stopped and waved or called out to her. It was almost comical the way their smiles disappeared when they saw me and Dad.

Lev pulled up to City Hall, and Adele gave him a gracious smile for the benefit of the people going into work. She smiled and waved at them, then turned with a pleasant expression on her face.

"Jonah and Lev, you all set? And Ashlyn, have a great day at work." She took a step closer to the golf cart and lowered her voice. "I'll pick you up at nine-thirty tonight."

We all nodded, and Lev puttered off.

"Do we have time to stop at the bungalow?" I asked Dad. "I kind of want a shower."

Dad shook his head. "No. I've never been late opening the warehouse, and I don't want today to be the day."

I sighed and sat back. I was also hoping to talk to Cyra. I hoped she had made it home okay. But I guess I didn't have time to worry about that. I'd have to settle for seeing her when it was all over.

Lev gave Dad a huge grin. "I can't wait to see the distribution warehouse. It has been on my bucket list for years."

I narrowed my eyes. "Are you lying?"

He laughed. "Yes, of course. I was just trying to psych myself up for a long day of boring numbers."

Dad looked offended, and I laughed along with Lev. He was right. This was going to be a long day.

CHAPTER 22

I regretted the plan exactly thirty seconds after Adele picked me up. In the excitement of planning the mission, I had forgotten that there would be downtime where it was just me and her.

So. Much. Downtime.

I clasped my hands together and tried to see through the darkness as Adele drove us to Weather Production.

"You don't like me, do you?"

Adele's voice startled me. I defaulted to deflection. "What do you mean?"

She snorted. "Come on. Be honest."

I decided I had nothing to lose. "I don't know you. The first thing I learned about you was that you were in total cahoots with Chip, the man who has wedged his way into my family. So I guess that means I didn't like you at the start. Now, I'm not sure what to think. It's hard to do a one-eighty to grasping that you're on our side."

Adele sighed. "I admit, I wish I had handled things differently." She was silent for a long moment, and I wondered how I was supposed to respond to that. "I have had to put on a front for so long that it just became second nature. My dad and grandpa expected me to act that way, and for the sake of the team, I did what was expected."

Her voice softened. "This is going to work because of how I've acted. No one will stop us, because no one will even dream that I would be part of something like this. You see?"

I hated to admit it, but I understood. The very reason I had a hard time trusting her was the reason she had the unwavering confidence of the town. My heart softened as I realized she was about to give it all up.

Adele pulled up to the gate in front of Weather Production, and the security lights popped on, blinding me for a second. But the security booth was empty. Adele hopped out of the golf cart and into the booth, and seconds later, the gate opened.

"Where is the guard?" I asked when she got back in the seat.

"We don't staff it at night. There's no need."

I snorted. "Because of your 'iron pills?'"

She gave me a sideways glance. "Yes. And as distasteful as I know you think that is, it's working out for us right now, isn't it?"

I grunted and held onto the side pole as Adele whipped the golf cart around the back of the building. She parked next to a door that was practically hidden by two manicured hedges and walked up and put her hand on a scanner. The door popped open.

I hurried in behind her. "Was that wise? Using your hand to get in? I mean, won't they trace this back to you?"

She gave me a funny look. "Well, since they're going to notice that the hurricane is gone, I've always assumed they'd trace it back to me. It's not like we can hide that."

My respect for her grew three sizes, just like the Grinch's heart. She really was willing to risk everything for this mission.

Adele walked down the halls like she owned the place. I chuckled to myself when I realized that she *did* own the place. She led me deep into the center of the building, pushing through two more checkpoints that required a hand scan for entry.

The control room was exactly what I expected. It was a large, open space with screens covering the walls. A work station was positioned in front of each screen. Only two people were present, a man and a woman, standing at two tall podiums that stood opposite each other near the center of the room.

They both turned at the sound of the door hissing open. I froze, a knee-jerk reaction to being caught in a building I wasn't supposed to be in.

The woman looked shocked for a second, but covered it with a smile. "Ms. Renwick! We weren't expecting you tonight. Uh, what brings you by?"

Adele put on the charming smile that told everyone she was in charge. "Oh, Ashlyn here wanted to see what it took to keep Goliath going at night."

The woman exchanged uneasy glances with the man. "What it takes? She's an outsider, ma'am."

Adele's stare turned frosty. "That's right, Belanna. Very good. And you think I shouldn't be showing her this?"

A stricken look covered Belanna's face. "No! I mean, obviously you can show anyone anything."

Adele walked over and put her arm around Belanna's shoulders. "Don't worry, Sweetie. Why don't you take a break? I think they restocked the break room with the cookies that everyone here likes. You and Gray should go put your feet up for a while."

Gray perked up. "There are cookies? I mean, are you sure? We're not supposed to take breaks on shift."

Adele's eyes twinkled. "Not unless someone who knows what to do can take over for you. But I'm here. I can handle your thirty-minute break."

Gray grinned, but Belanna still looked unsure. "Thirty minutes?"

Adele nodded. "Yes. And not a minute sooner, okay? I know how long these night shifts can be, and you deserve a break."

Relief relaxed Belanna's face. "Okay. Thank you so much, Ms. Renwick."

Adele kept a reassuring smile on her face until the door hissed shut behind Belanna and Gray after they exited. She then rushed to the door and pressed a button on the panel, and a lock clicked into place.

"Okay, quick tour," she said. "That station over there regulates and monitors the input from the energy harvesters. These three control the laser pillars. This is used to produce extra events, like the tornados. And the podiums in the center act as master controllers, one for the north side and one for the south side. At night, we only need to man the podiums to keep everything steady. During the day, teams are working in their individual sections to run diagnostics and make adjustments."

One station caught my eye. "What is that?"

"That's communications. It's the station used to contact USHA. Or anywhere."

My heart pounded. "That one can call out? Like, right now?"

Adele turned and gave me an intense stare. "Yes. But we don't have time for that, do we? In ten minutes, you and I have to enter the codes at the podiums at the exact same time, or the pillar teams won't be able to shut down the lasers."

Ten minutes seemed like a long time. I could get someone in that time and let them know I was okay. Maybe even what we were doing.

"Adele, *please.*" My eyes filled with tears. "I have to talk to someone in my family. I can't be this close and not try."

Compassion filled her face. "I know you want to. But in fifteen minutes, everything is going to change. You can contact them as soon as the mission is over. I promise. Besides, it's the middle of the night in Colorado, right? They'll be sleeping. We don't have time for you to try to wake them up. I need your focus now. Please, come over here so I can show you what to do."

I gave a longing look at the communication station. It wasn't even midnight at home yet. Trig would be awake still. Or Dasha. But Adele was right. I could wait fifteen more minutes.

I took a deep breath. "Okay. Let's do this."

Adele grinned. "Good. Because I'll need to go grab something from my office, but I want to show you first, so we're ready."

My blood ran cold. "You have time for that, but I don't have time to call home?"

She sighed. "We need it for the mission. Come on."

I gritted my teeth and stepped up to the podium. "Fine."

"When there is one minute left, I'll put my palm here first to wake up the restricted pad. Then I'll jump over to the other podium and do the same. The pad stays active for ten seconds, then will shut down if no codes are entered, so you'll need to type within ten seconds. Got it?"

My heart pounded. "But don't we have to do it at the same time?"

"We have to hit the final sequence at the same time. There are three codes. I'll call them out so we can do them together. You'll punch the code, then hit enter at the end of each. When we enter the final code, a button that says 'execute' will pop up. That's the one that can have no error."

I took a deep breath in through my nose to slow my breathing. "Okay."

Adele smiled at me. "This is it. We can do this. And then you'll call home, okay?"

I nodded, excitement flooding through my veins. "I can't believe this is all it takes."

She let out a short laugh. "Yeah, it only takes seven teams working at the exact same time. No big deal, right? Okay, so stay put. The codes we need are in a locked box in the Mayor's office right next door to this room. I'll be back in three minutes."

My stomach twisted. "Why didn't we stop there first?"

Adele was already backing toward the door. "I don't have time to explain. Just stay put, okay?"

I had no choice, so I nodded. She pressed her palm to the panel, and the door unlocked, then hissed open. She slipped out, and I breathed easier when I heard the lock click back into place behind her. The last thing I needed was for Gray or Belanna to walk back in here.

I stared at the massive monitors on the walls. This would be the last time I saw the live, swirling images of that wretched storm.

I glanced at the clock embedded in the wall. We had five minutes until our mark. I looked back at the door one more time, then rushed over to the communication station.

I pressed a few keys, and a number pad illuminated on the side of the small monitor. For a second, I panicked. All the contact info for everyone I knew was stored on my com, which was still locked in the storage facility in Colorado. But then Trig's com number filled my brain.

I laughed out loud. "Thanks, Mella." Mella had made me recite the com numbers for her, Trig, and Penn almost every night for a year when I had turned twelve. She always said that someday my com might run out of charge, and I would need to use someone else's to call home. We had stopped the practice, but Trig's number had etched itself into my long-term memory.

I punched in the number and glanced once more at the clock, my heart pounding. Adele would be back any second, but maybe Trig would pick up and I could see him for a moment. I stood ready to run back to the podium the minute I heard the lock click open.

The tone of a call came softly over the speakers at the station. I had no idea how to turn up the sound, and I didn't have time to look.

"Hello?" Trig's sleepy voice answered. The screen stayed dark. He had hit audio only. Mella would have been proud; she said to never allow video chat for an unknown number.

My voice became choked for a second. "Trig?" I squeaked out.

"Hello? Ash?"

"Yes! It's me! Turn on your camera!"

"Ashlyn! Hang on!" The screen flicked on, and Trig's face appeared on the screen. His face looked spooky, lit up only by the light of his com. His room was dark.

Tears poured down my face. "Trig! I only have two seconds, but I'm fine and we're about to turn off Goliath."

"What? Wait, tell me what's going on."

I shook my head. "I can't. Just listen fast. I found Dad. He's here. Chip has been behind everything. We're turning off the storm. Go turn on the news app. You'll see."

The sound of the lock clicked, and the door hissed.

I leaned close to the screen. "I have to go. I'll call you soon, okay?"

Trig panicked. "No, wait!"

I hit the button to turn off the screen and tried to walk calmly back to the podium.

Adele rushed in and locked the door behind her. "Got it. Ready?"

I took a deep breath and nodded. "Let's do this."

She put a piece of paper on her podium, then stepped over to mine, her eyes on the clock.

"Here we go in three, two, one." She pressed her palm on the screen, and the code pad popped up. It was an entire keyboard and number pad.

"Okay, ready?"

This was it.

"R-D-7-2-V-V-R."

She called out the code at an even pace, and I punched in the letters and numbers. A green box appeared to the right of the code pad.

"It's green!" I yelled.

"Great. Now, X-3-P-9-9-F-1."

A second green box appeared.

"Got it."

"7-1-9-S-Q-6-G."

The red Execute box appeared.

"Hold on," Adele shouted. "Hit that in three, two, one, *now*."

I pressed the red box and held my breath as I stared at the largest monitor on the wall.

"Did it work?"

She didn't answer, her eyes glued to the monitor above the pillar monitoring station. The six lights of the stations flicked from green to red, one by one.

The lock clicked, and the door hissed open, and we whirled around to face the door. Two men entered. They were both older than Adele, although one looked downright ancient.

"Well, what's going on in here, young lady?"

"Dad. Grandpa."

My heart sank. These were Geno and Ashton Renwick? Ashton, the creator of Goliath. I couldn't believe that such a destructive, wicked storm came from this man who looked like the kind of grandpa everyone wished to have. Distinguished, yet trim and fit, ready to keep up with everyone.

Ashton took a step forward. "What have you done?"

Adele raised her chin. "I'm pretty sure you know, or you wouldn't be here. How did you find out?"

He chuckled. "Pax, of course. His little girlfriend has always been such a wealth of information." His laughter stopped. "Of course, Pax hasn't always been very reliable. If only he had come to us an hour sooner."

Cyra? This was my fault. I should have known how upset she was about not being included on the teams. I should have insisted on finding her, rather than going to the warehouse with Dad. I clenched my fists and glanced at the screens. The deep purple of the outer ring of Goliath had already turned red. It was downgrading.

"Adele," I said. "I think it worked."

The men seemed to finally notice that I was there. "You must be Ashlyn. The little thorn in the side of so many," Ashton boomed out.

Geno stepped over to the communication station and pushed some buttons.

I shrugged. "You guys are too late. We did it. We shut down Goliath."

Ashton's face filled with rage. "No, what you did was make a mess of everything. Everything had to be hit at the same time, and you missed one. All you did was doom a lot of people."

Adele turned pale. "What do you mean?"

"I mean, we were only able to get to one team. One pillar is still active."

I looked at Adele in horror. "But that means the storm is still active."

"That's right," Ashton said. "Active, and now moving. And where is it going? Well, no one knows. All you did was unleash a beast on innocent people."

All the screens in the room blipped black for a second, then came back on. I gasped.

Chips's face was on every screen.

And Mom sat next to him.

CHAPTER 23

I DIDN'T THINK. I just ran to the communication station.

"Mom!" I leaned in close to the monitor, tears streaming down my face. "Are you okay?"

She leaned in, her mouth open. "Ashlyn? Oh, Ash! Honey, where are you?"

I wiped my cheeks. "I'm in the Eye. And Dad is here. Mom, Chip has been lying to you this whole time. He knew Dad was here."

A small part of me wondered if I should be careful with my words, with Chip sitting right next to her, but there was no time.

Mom's face paled, and she turned to Chip. "Is this true?"

He set his mouth. "I've never seen him, so I was never sure. That's the truth, Livvy."

I snorted. "It's a half truth. He knew Dad was here, because he's been working with the Renwicks the whole time."

Chip cleared his throat. "Now is not the time for this. Ashlyn, I told you what would happen if you interfered. And yet, you just couldn't seem to help yourself, could you?"

I clenched my fists. "You know how proud you are to be the Hurricane Keeper? Well, I am the Storm Breaker."

Mom's face clouded with anger, a familiar sight that always made me, Mella, Trig, and Penn slip away as soon as possible. "Chip, you need to tell me what is going on. Right now."

Chip stared into the monitor, somehow making eye contact with me. "Ashlyn has shifted the storm. Everything we've ever worked for is about to be destroyed. All your careful, well-organized handling of the energy production is about to be shattered. Isn't that right, Ash?"

Rage clawed at my throat. "Destroyed? You mean, *set right*. This storm should never have happened, and USHA needs to answer for the death and destruction it's caused."

Chip snorted. "USHA didn't cause it. USHA simply found a way to live with it, and use its energy to benefit society. And you, in your foolish, youthful mind, unilaterally decided to strip away your country of the benefits. When this story gets out, I won't be the villain. You will be."

Ashton stepped up behind me. "Oh, you'll have plenty to answer for, Chip. You are in breach of contract."

Chip scowled. "It's obvious this wasn't my fault, Renwick."

Ashton snorted. "You let your personal feelings cloud your judgment. I told you that any problems that came up needed to be dealt with permanently. The Bookers should have never made it to the Eye, yet you went soft."

Chip leaned in closer to the monitor, his voice low. "The Eye should have contained them. Tell me, did that rag tag team of Storm Chasers really manage to figure out how to shut this down in the two weeks that they were there? Or did someone on your side give them what they needed?"

Ashton turned his anger toward Geno. "That will be dealt with."

For the first time, Geno showed some life as he clenched his fists and faced his father. "You're going to blame *me* for this? I trained Adele the same way you trained me."

Adele stepped forward. "Your old-school ways of thinking were going to kill the City, Grandpa. Your eugenics program and experiments are what alerted me to the fact that none of this should have happened."

"Enough!" Mom's firm, don't-mess-with-me voice boomed over the speakers, and everyone jumped. "I can't believe what I'm hearing. And I'm going to put a stop to it." She stood, and Chip grabbed her arm and pulled her down. Hard. I gasped at his manhandling.

"Get your hands off of her, dirtbag!" I shouted.

Mom tried to yank her arm away, but Chip held on, a wild look in his eye. "What happens to you next is Ashlyn's fault," he told her. "She had simple instructions to just let everything be, but she couldn't even follow those. Maybe if you had been a better mother, she would have learned obedience."

Mom pulled her hand back and slapped Chip with a power I hadn't seen. I pumped my fist in the air. "Yes!"

A low roar filled the room, and the walls rattled. Glass shattered somewhere outside the room as the screens flickered. Belanna and Gray came bursting in, their eyes wide with fright. They stopped short when they saw who was in the control room.

"Oh my gosh. Mr. Renwick!" Belanna said, her mouth wide open.

Gray was the only one who seemed focused on the next steps. "Sirs, we have to evacuate. I think Goliath has moved.

The eyewall has already swept over the southern border, and will be here any moment."

Geno looked panicked. "This building is not designed to withstand a hurricane."

Ashton swore. "No, the best we can do is wait it out. This room should be adequate, and Goliath should move on."

Belanna ran to the center podium and punched a few keys. The radar image of Goliath popped back up. "Sir, it looks like it's still tethered to the west pillar. Will it be able to move on?"

My heart sank. That was the pillar that Dad was assigned to. I clenched my fists and turned to Ashton.

"That's where Dad is! What did you do?" I shouted.

For the first time, Ashton looked at a loss. "I didn't know who was there. I just sent a team in to detain whoever breached the entrance."

Geno stepped next to Belanna. "Can you shut down that pillar?"

Ashton took a shaky step forward. "No!"

Geno turned. "Dad, we have to let it go. If we can untether it, it'll move out to the Atlantic and dissolve. If we don't, it'll destroy the City, and then more of the southeastern section of the United States. Maybe even the entire East coast."

"No!" Chip roared, his grip tightening on Mom's arm. "You can't do this. Everything I've worked for will be ruined. All the good that the US has developed."

Mom glared at him. "Your 'good' was built on lies. It's not good."

Geno set his mouth. "Belanna, shut it down. Let it go."

Belanna looked between Ashton and Geno, her face stricken.

Adele stepped forward. "Belanna, do it. I'm the reigning mayor. It's my call. Shut down the pillar."

Belanna swallowed hard, then nodded at Gray. He stepped up to his podium, and Belanna called out a series of commands that they typed in together. Everyone in the command center turned to watch the radar. Within seconds, the swirling mass of Goliath inched toward the northeast.

The roar of the winds became louder, and the screens flickered again.

"Freeze! Police!"

We all jumped and looked toward the door before realizing that the sound came over the speakers.

Chip and Mom both looked off screen. A look of disbelief had covered Chip's face.

"Put your hands where I can see them! Both of you."

Satisfaction covered Mom's face as she yanked her arm away from Chip, this time breaking free. She put her hands in the air and sat calmly while Chip appeared to refuse.

"Gentlemen, do you know who I am?" Chip demanded.

"Yes, sir. Hands in the air. We won't ask again."

Chip growled and grudgingly obeyed. "Fine, but I hope you have a back-up plan for when you lose your badge in the morning."

Mom leaned away from Chip. "Officer, he's holding me here against my will. And he kidnapped my daughter."

Chip let out a laugh. "She's crazy. You know we're dating, right? She asked me to come here in the middle of the night so we could fool around in my office. She loves the feeling of power."

Mom looked like she wanted to throw up. If it hadn't been so disgusting, I would have laughed. Finally, Mom was getting to see his true colors. My heart turned over as her face turned bright red. I know she must have been so embarrassed. I wanted to tell her it wasn't her fault.

"Sir, you have the right to remain silent. Anything you—"

The power shut off in the room and we plunged into darkness. I crouched down and covered my head, the roar of Goliath now deafening.

All I could do was sit there and pray. I had no idea what happened to anyone else. Clearly, Luca and Miri were successful. All the teams were, except for Dad. What happened to him? Was he hurt? Were all the other teams safe from Goliath?

I prayed Mom was safe and that Chip really was being arrested. Would he find a way to worm his way out of this?

A loud crash sounded out in the hall, and I crawled toward the communication station to hide under the desk. At least, I hoped I was crawling in the right direction. I had never been in such darkness. I tried to keep one hand extended out in front of me, glad that I did when I found the chair in my path.

An even louder crash sounded in the command center room, and a woman shrieked. I couldn't tell if it was Adele or Belanna. I willed my eyes to adjust, but there was total blackness.

A calm came over me as I realized that I probably wouldn't survive this. I had seen what Goliath had done to the disaster zone. And we had tried to shut it down while it was at the height of its power, which means the eyewall bearing down on the City was the strongest one the world had ever seen. The destruction would be complete. It would mow down the City as if everything were made of crumbs to be swept off the table with the brush of a hand.

But I had done it. I found Dad. He was alive, just like I said. And I helped the Storm Chasers stop the storm. The world would soon know the truth about the storm. How could they not, when they woke up in the morning and the storm was gone? They would look to USHA, and USHA would have to tell the truth. Hopefully, everyone would understand the need for more accountability in our government.

And I had gotten to see Trig one more time. And Mom. I let the tears fall that had welled up. I would have loved to hug them both one more time, but I could be content with seeing their faces and knowing that they now knew the truth about me and Dad.

And Mom had seen the truth about Chip. I realized I didn't care what happened to him as long as Mom got away from him. Although it would have been so fun to watch him go through a very public trial, and then answer for his crimes.

The only regret I had left was that I didn't get to see Dasha one more time. I knew Trig would tell her, and I even knew she would probably forgive me. But I wished I could have heard about the Seattle trip. And how everything worked out with Rosalie and Zed.

I prayed Luca would make it out. His mom was still in Canada; maybe he could go stay with her until he figured out what to do with his life.

I really hoped Dad was still alive, too. I let my mind wander and imagine what the reunion between Dad and

Mom would be like. I'm sure they would have things to work out, but Mom would forgive him, now that she knew how involved Chip was in Dad's disappearance.

Another loud crack sounded, followed by the sound of splintering wood. Something hit my head. The roar of the wind turned into a high-pitched ringing, and then the sounds just faded away.

CHAPTER 24

A HAND SQUEEZED MINE. I tried to squeeze back, but an intense ache filled my head. Nausea overwhelmed me, so I tried to roll onto my side, groaning at the stabbing pain at the top of my head.

"Shh. Lay still." A woman's soothing voice, nice and soft. I didn't recognize it.

I tried to open my eyes, but squeezed them shut. The light was too bright.

"Jonah." The woman said.

"Oh, thank goodness." I winced at the loudness of Dad's voice.

"Shh," the woman said. "Speak softly. Loud sounds and bright lights aren't good for her right now. You sit with her, and I'll check if one of the med chambers is available."

"Dad?" I whispered without opening my eyes.

"Yeah, sweetie. I'm here." His voice was choked, and he grabbed my hand.

"You made it?"

"Yeah, sweetie. I'm okay. We're all okay. Luca's okay."

My heart turned over, grateful that he knew to say that.

I swallowed. "I saw Mom."

"You did?"

I tried to nod, but it hurt. "Yeah. And Trig. I got to call them."

Dad squeezed my hand. "That's good. I think we'll get to see them soon."

"Did it work?"

"The mission? Yeah. Goliath's gone. And so is most of the City."

I tried to open my eyes. The lights were just so bright.

"No, don't do that. Lie still."

I forced one eye open. "No, I want to see."

"I'll tell you. You're at the Med Center. It's a real mess, but the med centers were fortified pretty well. We think the Renwicks had them designed that way in order to protect them. And it worked out for us. They've been able to treat the survivors. You're next, honey. As soon as a chamber becomes available, they'll fix that concussion in a blink of an eye."

I squeezed my eyes shut. "I'm so tired."

He brushed the hair off of my face, and I winced as his fingers grazed a tender spot on my head. "Oops, sorry. You took a nasty hit right there. Rest, sweet pea. We'll chat when you're done with your treatment."

The sound of his voice and the feel of his touch faded away as I drifted off again. I woke to the calming scent of vanilla and lavender. I opened my eyes and realized that I felt great. Like I had when I came out of the refresher. Was that only a couple of days ago?

I was in one of the refresher rooms.

"Your refresher has ended. Please get dressed and head to the lobby." My old friend, the automated voice urged me on.

I grinned and stretched. "Thanks. I will."

I dressed in my clothes that were covered in dirt and what looked like dried blood, then hurried out into the hall, stopping short. The hall was filled with people sitting around, waiting for their turn in the room. They looked like they had been through a battle. Or a disaster, I guess. They all looked shell-shocked. A few were crying.

A woman tried to comfort a little girl. "Momma, are we getting invaded? Are they gonna steal all of our stuff now?"

The mom stroked the girl's head. "Sweetheart, don't worry. It doesn't matter. What matters is we're going to stay together, okay? I won't let anyone take you from me."

The girl sniffed and buried her head in her mom's chest. The mom leaned her head back on the wall, her eyes bright with fear. Anger burned in my chest. The Renwicks had done this. They had filled their citizens with lies and fear to keep them in line, and now these poor people thought they were going to be captured and enslaved or something.

I picked my way through the hall, making sure to not step on anyone, and made it to the lobby. It was just as packed as the halls. Runa was at the desk, looking stressed as she handed out room assignments. I thought about stopping to see her, but I caught sight of Dad standing by the door. He rubbed his head like he had a headache.

"Dad!"

His head shot up, and the worried lines on his face relaxed. "Ash. Thank goodness."

I rushed to him, and he wrapped me in a tight hug. But I pushed away after a moment. "Where's everyone else?"

He put his arm around me and guided me toward the door. His eyes were filled with a sadness that scared me. "Outside. Come on. There's a lot you need to catch up on."

The world outside the med center was nothing like it was before. All the lush, perfect landscaping looked like it had been scraped over. Palm trees and fronds had been snapped and tossed carelessly around. The buildings across the street looked like a giant had smashed each one of them on his way down the street.

The sun was shining brightly, as if this were just the start of a lovely May day. The blue sky had just traces of thin clouds lazily drifting across the sky.

The dark eyewall of Goliath was gone.

I gripped Dad's hand like I was eight years old again. Without the eyewall surrounding us, I felt exposed. It was amazing how quickly I had gotten used to the powerful boundary around us. If I felt this way after just two weeks inside the eye, how must the people feel who had lived here their whole lives?

Dad led me around the side of Med Center, and I saw Luca and the entire team sitting at a few of the cement tables that had survived Goliath's path. Miri saw me and touched Luca on the shoulder. Luca's eyes shot up, and he jumped up and ran at us.

Dad glanced at me with a slight grin and let go of my hand just before Luca scooped me up in a tight hug. He twirled me around, then set me on the ground, grabbed my face, and kissed me with surprising tenderness. I didn't even care everyone was watching.

At least, not until I heard them all cheering.

I broke away from Luca, my face heating. I shyly looked in to his eyes, and he winked at me before grabbing my hand.

"Hey, Booker."

"Hey, Denzio."

He laughed. "I can't believe you made it. I thought for sure you were dead. I mean, the Weather Production building was a mess."

That didn't make sense. "It was? Then how did I get out?"

He shrugged. "They found you outside the building. You don't remember going outside?"

I rubbed the top of my head, wondering how hard I had been hit. "No. We were in the command center, which was in the very center of the building. Ashton said it was the safest place. Everything went black, and I crawled under a desk. It was so loud in there. And then I woke up here. Did they find anyone else?"

Luca's face turned grim. "Come on. Let's debrief."

We joined the rest of the Storm Breakers, and I realized that not everyone had made it back. Ginger, Silas, Hugh, Jack, and Miri were there. So were Annette, Lisha, Lev and Georgie. But Cyra and Adele were missing.

"Where's Cyra?" I asked.

Jack looked glum. "She's okay. She's with her parents, trying to salvage stuff from their house. It got totally smashed."

My heart dropped. "But Gwen and Xander are okay?"

He nodded. "It's a miracle, though. Everyone was sleeping in that drugged state when Goliath swept through, so Cyra had a terrible time waking them up to take shelter."

I pressed my lips together. "She told Pax about our plan. He told Ashton and Geno, and they sent a team to stop us.

That's why we weren't able to completely shut down the pillars, and why Goliath moved instead of fizzled."

Jack's face grew pale. "I don't think she knew that. I know her. She wouldn't have tried to stop us. I think she was just venting to Pax."

Ginger and Silas sat close together. Silas had his head in his hands. I gave Ginger a questioning look.

"Matteo's dead," she whispered.

My mouth dropped open. "What? Are you sure?"

Dad leaned on the table. "I saw it. Matteo was at the pillar Lev and I were supposed to hit. At first I thought he was there to stop us, because he was trying to stop us from going in. He was waving a gun at us and telling us to hurry. Then a team of soldiers showed up. I don't know how they knew."

"Pax," I growled. "Cyra told Pax. He told his great-grandpa, and Ashton sent them to stop you."

Dad ran his hand through his hair. "Well, it worked. Matteo shouted for us to hurry, that he'd hold them off for as long as possible, and he started shooting at them. They fired back. Lev and I took cover, and we saw Matteo get hit." Dad's voice broke. "It was a head shot. Matteo dropped and didn't move. Right then, the storm shifted. Lev and I were the closest to the base of the pillar, so we made it inside to take shelter. By the time we got back outside, everyone was gone, including Matteo. There's no way he could have survived. I think his body was blown away by Goliath."

Silas spoke up in a gravelly voice. "Are you sure Matteo was trying to help you?"

Dad's eyes filled with tears. "Yeah. He put himself between us and the soldiers."

Silas sniffed and nodded. "Thanks. I needed to hear that."

Ginger looped her arm through Silas' and rested her head on his shoulder. A rock formed in my stomach. As much as I hated Matteo for what he said to my dad to keep him in the eye for this long, and for luring us here, that wasn't an end that I wished on him.

"And Adele?" I asked.

Dad shook his head. "No one has seen her."

I swallowed. "Ashton and Geno Renwick were in the command center with us. Any news on them?"

Georgie sighed. "There's no news on anyone right now. Not even Dad." She wiped her eyes. "But I'm not expecting anything good. There's no way the farm could have survived that."

My heart twisted as I looked around. Was it the right thing to do, shutting Goliath down like that? Was it worth it? Most of the people of the City weren't to blame. The Renwicks had drugged and conditioned them to believe lies, but they weren't the ones who were in charge. And we just mowed over their lives in order to fulfill our own agenda.

Did that make me like Chip and Ashton? Willing to ruin lives, just so what I believed should happen could happen?

The sound of a commotion erupted near the entrance of the med center. We all ran over just in time to see the med vans unloading stretchers. Ashton lay lifeless on one, and Geno was on the other.

"It's the Renwicks!" someone shouted.

The crowd parted, pulling their own families out of the way so Ashton and Geno could get in to the med chambers as soon as possible.

I shook my head. "These people really love their mayors, don't they?"

Dad put his arm around my shoulders. "All they've known their whole lives is that the Renwicks took care of them. They gave them top-notch medical care and protected them from a world filled with criminals and monsters. They had no reason to not believe everything they've ever been told."

I folded my arms across my chest. "And was it the right thing to do to shut them down like this? I mean, should we have warned everyone in the City about what we planned to do, so they could take proper shelter?"

Dad sighed. "I don't know, honey. I don't know if they would have hunkered down or tried to stop us."

The crowd outside became quiet. Even the breeze died down. It was as if everyone were holding their breath, sitting vigil for the Renwicks. After a few silent minutes, people talked in indistinct murmurs, holding each other and speaking words of comfort.

Even our team was frozen. We stood at a respectful distance from the med center entrance, but we needed to know what was going to happen. After about fifteen minutes, Runa stepped out of the med center. Her face was red and streaked.

"Ashton is gone," she sniffed. "And we still don't know about Geno. He's not responding to the med chamber, but he's still alive."

A collective gasp rose from the crowd, and a few women burst into tears.

I turned to our group. "Well? What do we do now?"

Silas shrugged. "I think we have to wait to see what happens to Geno. We need at least one of the Renwicks. They're going to have to answer some questions."

Panic clawed up my throat. Getting rid of Goliath wasn't enough. With no one to give a testimony about what truly happened, Chip could deny everything. "And no one has seen Adele?"

Everyone looked at each other helplessly.

She was the key. We had to find her.

I backed away from the group. "Well, then I'm going back to Weather Production. We have to find her."

"Wait!" Luca called. "We don't have any golf carts. They all got blown away by Goliath."

I froze for a second, then kept going. "Then I'll walk."

"Hang on, now," Georgie called out. "Work smarter, not harder. That's what Dad always said. We'll take the med van."

I stopped in surprise. "You can drive those?"

She grinned. "Haven't you learned every vehicle has the keys inside it? No one steals things in the Eye. We'll just hop on in. And it can take everyone, if you don't mind cramming in the back."

We didn't even have to discuss it. We all ran for the van and hopped in, Georgie jumping in the driver's seat.

She peeked over her shoulder. "Y'all set?"

We nodded, and Georgie drove forward, dodging people and debris in the road. We had to find Adele. Nothing else mattered.

CHAPTER 25

The devastation was unlike anything I had ever seen.

I thought I had gotten an understanding of what a hurricane could do when we drove through Goliath. But that wasn't true. All we saw through the storm was a landscape that had been scrubbed clean and bare. The occasional branches we came across were nothing.

The City had been a thriving metropolis full of life. And now there were piles of rubble, with people picking and sorting through what they could salvage.

I had no joy that Goliath was finally gone.

Georgie eased the van onto the long drive that led up to Weather Production, and I gasped. They had told me it was a mess, but I thought they were exaggerating.

They weren't.

It was like the building had been made of sticks, and the big bad wolf blew it away. Only, not completely. A structure that looked like the shelters out in the storm stood in the middle of the pile, as if the sticks had been laid down around it to pay homage.

I pointed. "That's the command center."

Silas grunted. "It makes sense that of all the buildings in this City, they'd construct only Weather Production and the med centers from materials that would withstand a hurricane."

I could see a path through the rubble that lead to a door in the structure. "That must be where the rescue workers dug to find Ashton and Geno."

I jumped out of the van and made my way to the door, pushing aside debris and being careful where I stepped. There were plenty of sharp nails and broken glass along the path. I peeked in the door, but it was hard to see. The roof had been smashed in, so a little light came in, but mostly it was as dark as it had been the last time I saw it.

"Do we have any flashlights?" I asked.

Ginger handed me one. "Be careful. We don't know how stable it is."

"Adele?" I called out. "Are you in there?"

I moved aside a board and stepped inside. Someone groaned dead ahead.

"I hear her! Come on!" I pushed my way through.

"Ashlyn, stop. Let me go," Dad said.

"You don't know the way. I've got this." I ducked under a fallen beam and made my way to the center of the room, where the podiums had stood. It took a minute, but I finally saw an arm sticking out from under some rubble. "Over here!"

Dad and Luca had been close behind me, and they began moving the larger pieces. I crouched down and touched the arm. "Adele?"

But then I realized it was a man's arm. "Gray?"

Gray coughed. "Yeah. I'm here."

"Oh, my gosh. Stay still. Hang on, we'll get you out."
Dad, Luca, Silas, and Jack had all made their way in. They

carefully removed each piece, moving slowly, just in case moving something caused more damage to Gray.

He gave a weak smile. "Thanks for coming back. I wasn't sure anyone would."

I touched his hair. "Did they know you were in here?"

"I guess not. But everyone was pretty upset when they found the Renwicks. I bet they just forgot to look for anyone else."

I glanced around at the wreckage. "Belanna?"

He shook his head. "I don't know. I haven't heard her."

Dad and Luca moved the last board, and Gray moved to sit up.

"No, wait," Dad said. "We don't know how hurt you are."

Gray tested his arms. "I think I might be okay. Okay enough to get to the Med Center, I mean."

I sighed and looked at the overwhelming damage in the room. "I don't know if we'll be able to find Adele."

Dad set his mouth. "We have to. Even if it's her body."

Dad and Luca helped Gray to his feet, supporting him as they made their way out to the med van. Georgie loaded him in and drove away.

Hugh took charge of the search and rescue plan. We started at the door and removed debris after Hugh deemed each piece safe enough. Dad and Luca would only let Miri and me in as far as they had checked to remove the smaller pieces of wreckage. Ginger picked through the rubble, trying to salvage any of the tech she could find. We wouldn't know if any of the information was recoverable until we could get somewhere to power it up, but she grabbed as many drives and tech pads as she could. The sun grew hot and the air stale and muggy, without the swirling winds of

Goliath around to keep the breeze steady and mild. Georgie returned with a few City people who were willing to help look for Adele.

We found Belanna near the edge of the command center. She didn't make it. Ginger thought she bled out internally from blunt force trauma. Guilt threatened to overwhelm me, but I kept working. We had to find Adele.

Georgie took Belanna's body to the Med Center and returned with bottles of water. We took a break, crowding together in the shade of the cement wall near the security booth. There wasn't much chatting. We were all too tired.

A distant rumble drew our attention to the southeast. The unmistakable orange fireball of a rocket appeared on the horizon, and a rocket shot up and toward the northwest.

My mouth dropped open. "Who was that? Ashton is dead."

Georgie's face filled with hope. "Maybe that was Adele."

That didn't make sense. "Adele? She left us? Without saying anything?"

Georgie shrugged. "Who else would go in the shuttles? No one knew about them."

Miri sat down and leaned against the wall, exhaustion on her face. "So, does that mean we're done?"

Silas rubbed the back of his neck. "I'd feel better if we finished clearing out the room. Then we'd know for sure."

Miri groaned. "But what if it's for nothing? I say let's stop and go back to the Med Center. If Adele is in that room, she's not going anywhere. If we find out she wasn't on that shuttle, we can come back."

My stomach was in knots. Panic crawled up my throat, and I hyperventilated.

Luca grabbed my hand. "Ash, what is it?"

I tried to look at him through tears. "What do we do now? We don't have Adele, and we don't have a way home. What have we done?"

"Hey!" Jack shouted, pointing at the sky.

Three dark helicopters swung over the City. Jack ran out to the road, waving his arms. The rest of us followed, doing the same. The copter circled twice, then flew back toward the Med Center.

Jack's face fell. "Dang. Why didn't they stop?"

Silas took charge. "Let's go back to the Med Center. Since that's where a lot of people are, I bet that's where any rescue started. Miri is right; we can come back and keep searching for Adele. Let's be honest; if she were alive, we would have heard her by now. So if it's just her body, it will still be here."

I looked at Dad. "What do we do? We need a Renwick."

He sighed. "Silas is right. We don't have to be gone long. But let's go find out about the helicopters. I bet they have a way of contacting home."

A rush of adrenaline surged through me, and finding Adele became less of a priority. How had I forgotten about home? I could call home now.

Just as we all started to load up the med van, the distinct chuffing of helicopter blades grew loud as they moved toward us. Jack ran back toward the road, as if he was the one who would guide the copter to us. The helicopter came in low and swung around. Hugh ran and grabbed Jack and pulled him back so the helicopter could land on the road.

We lined up near the wall, watching the helicopter as it touched down and bracing ourselves from the wind it made. The door of the copter slid open as the blades slowed down.

Trig jumped out.

I burst into tears and ran towards him. He ran and met me halfway, and I jumped into his arms, crying and laughing.

He pushed me back. "Ashlyn Grace! How dare you!"

I laughed as he tried to scold me and grabbed him in a hug again. He didn't smell the greatest, and I wondered when he had showered last. I gasped as Penn and Mella hopped out of the copter.

"Is Mom here?" I asked Trig.

Trig turned and Mom climbed out. She took one look at Trig and me, and ran like I had never seen her run before, Penn and Mella hot on her tail. We smashed together in a group hug, everyone laughing and crying. Penn rubbed my head in one of his special noogies, and Mella tried to put on her stern big sister face, but didn't quite make it work. Mom pushed Trig aside and grabbed my shoulders, looking me all over.

"Ashlyn, you're grounded," she said.

I laughed and wiped my nose. "That's fair."

Then she dropped her arms and took in a sharp breath. I looked over my shoulder to see Dad walking toward us.

Mella, Penn, and Trig all froze. I couldn't help it; I had something to say.

I stepped back between them and Dad and put my hands on my hips. "I told you he was alive."

Mom pushed past me and walked to Dad. Trig pulled me back and held me in place so Mom and Dad could talk.

They were just far enough away, and the hum of the helicopter engine was still loudly winding down, so we couldn't hear anything they were saying. Dad's face was ashen and filled with sorrow. All we could see was the back of Mom's head. I wanted to go over, but Trig held on to me.

"Stay here," he said.

Mella nodded and put her arm around my shoulders. "Ash, I'm so sorry. I didn't believe you."

I turned and gave her a smile. "It's okay, Mel. I'm not mad at you."

Her face was grim. "I'm mad at myself."

I looked at Trig. "How are you here?"

Trig's face twisted into anger, an expression I had rarely seen from my easy-going brother. "As soon as you cut off the call, I called Mom, but I couldn't get her. So I called the police and told them that my mom might be in danger. They sent a squad car to the house, but she wasn't there, which was weird since it was so late. So they went to USHA, and they found Mom and Chip in Chip's office. They arrested Chip on charges of kidnapping." His voice broke. "I'm so angry we let that guy into our house. Why didn't you tell us about him before?"

Tears filled my eyes again. "Because he said he'd hurt Mom and you if I ever did. And I believed him."

Mella hugged me. "Trig called and said to turn on the news app because you said Goliath was going away. So I did, even though you know I hate the news apps. But Goliath moved off into the Atlantic. Mom called us and told us to meet her at USHA, because we were leaving for Florida."

She broke off and clutched my arm. Mom and Dad were kissing in a desperate way that was both beautiful and awkward to watch. Penn gagged and pretended like he was going to vomit. I covered my mouth, and Mella turned all of us away to give them some privacy.

I broke out into a laugh. "Would you believe that's not the first old couple I've seen make out like that in the last few weeks?"

Mella wrinkled her nose. "We want to hear everything, but maybe not about that."

I smiled and nodded back toward the Storm Chasers, who were still lined up against the wall, watching everything. "I have so much to tell you, but first, we're trying to find Adele Renwick. She's the mayor of the City. Her grandfather was Ashton Renwick, the one who captured Goliath. Ashton died when Goliath swept over the City, and her dad is still in a coma or something. But we have to find Adele, so she can tell the rest of the world what really went on here."

Trig looked at Mella. "Adele? Is that the lady they said already left for Buckley?"

My mouth dropped open. "Are you sure?"

Mella shrugged. "The rescue teams said that a City leader named Adele had given them instructions on where to find people, and that she had her own way out of the City."

Penn's face was a thundercloud. "How long have they had rocket shuttles?"

I sighed. "It's a long story."

Mella brightened. "I think Mom and Dad are done."

I turned, and Mom and Dad walked toward us with their arms around each other. I stepped aside to let Dad reconnect with Mella, Trig, and Penn. I wrapped my arms around Mom's waist, and she hugged me back.

"Ashlyn, I thought I lost you."

I nodded. "I know. I'm so sorry. I thought this was the way it had to go."

She shook her head and laughed a little. "You've always been so much like your dad. I should have known."

I pushed back. "What about Chip?"

Her face bloomed red. "I'm so mad about that. And embarrassed."

I squeezed her. "No, don't be. I know you made the choices you thought you had to make. You just didn't have all the information."

She let out a heavy sigh. "Well, right now Chip's being held by federal authorities. I hope for a long time. They're diving deep into USHA in a way I never did. I had no idea. I'm so ashamed."

"There is no shame in not knowing something. You aren't responsible for information you never had."

Mom laughed and pressed her cheek to my head. "You sound like Trig's therapy app."

I sighed. "I think it's time for me to sign up for that app."

She nodded. "I'm sure."

Dad turned to me and Mom, his arms around Mella, Trig, and Penn, and tears in his eyes. "So, can we go home?"

Mom nodded. "This is our ride."

I glanced back at the team. "Can they come too?"

She smiled. "We have more choppers. We came to get all the Storm Chasers out."

Dad grunted. "I guess you'll want that boy to come with us, though."

Trig's mouth dropped open. "What boy?"

I grinned as my cheeks heated. "Uh, I have a lot to tell you guys."

Epilogue

I LOVED THE WAY the temperature dropped as soon as the sun disappeared behind the mountains. We should have known that picking the fourth of July for my graduation party would mean we were picking the hottest day of the year in Colorado. But our backyard was finally cooling off, and I had picked the best spot for viewing the firework show that would shoot off of the top of Castle Rock.

Luca sank into the chair next to mine, and I reached for his hand. He gave me his cutest half-grin as he intertwined his fingers with mine. "Nice party, Booker."

I rolled my eyes. "This is for Mom and Dad. They're celebrating that their last child is out of high school and launching into the world."

Dasha plopped down in the chair on the other side of me. "Oh, stop. This is for you, since you missed the party we were supposed to have together." My heart flipped over, and I opened my mouth, but she held up her hand. "Stop. I'm not guilt tripping you. Besides, my graduation party was so lame. This one is way better."

I smiled. "Then this party is for you, too." I grabbed my com and opened the house display app. The message on the screen outside the house changed from "Congratulations Ashlyn" to "Congrats Ash and Dash."

Dasha laughed and leaned back in her chair, settling in for the wait for the fireworks. I studied her face for a minute, looking for any sign of anger, but it wasn't there. I think she really forgave me for ditching her on our senior trip. Which was great, because we planned to room together at UCCS.

I had to stop myself from laughing out loud. Mason was the one who suggested that I go to the University of Colorado at Colorado Springs, so I could be close to him while he was in the Air Force Academy. It felt so weird that I was actually going there, but not for that reason. UCCS had a great meteorology tech program, and I wanted to get the degree I needed so I could work with Dad and Mom. It also had the interior design program that Dasha wanted, so it made the most sense for us to go together.

Dad stood near our back deck, still flipping burgers and turning hot dogs. He laughed and joked with Penn, who hadn't left Dad's side since we got back. Penn and Trig had even moved back home. They said they could find another apartment later. Mom and Mella were busy directing the food, making sure that all bowls and plates were filled.

"Whoa," Luca said. He tugged on my hand and pointed to the side gate. Hugh had just entered the backyard with Georgie. And they were holding hands.

My mouth dropped open. "What is happening?"

Hugh caught sight of us and tugged Georgie in our direction.

"Hey, guys. Happy graduation, Ashlyn," he said.

I narrowed my eyes and pointed at their clasped hands. "Forget that. When did this happen?"

Georgie blushed. "Uh, there's nothing like doing a dangerous mission to bring people together."

I laughed. "Oh, this is awesome. I'm so happy for you!"

Hugh looked at Georgie, smitten. "We would have never met if I hadn't gone to the Eye. So the credit goes to you, Ashlyn, for helping us get there."

I waved away the comment. "How's your dad?"

Georgie's mouth twisted. "He's hanging in there. He still refuses to get into a med chamber, so he's recovering from his broken hip the old-fashioned way. He's in a rehab center in Baton Rouge. He didn't want to leave the South."

I sighed. "Is it rude to say that I'm so glad he just has a broken hip? It could have been so much worse."

Goliath had flattened Miko's farm, but somehow the old men hanging out there had survived by huddling together in the center of the old farmhouse. None of the chickens made it, though.

Georgie clutched Hugh's hand tighter. "I'm glad, too. We're, ah, going to visit him next week, so we can tell him our news in person." She held out her left hand, displaying a small, beautiful engagement ring.

Luca's eyebrows shot up, and he jumped out of his chair. "Hugh! Whoa, you didn't waste any time, buddy!"

Hugh shrugged. "Why would I wait? Crazy stuff has happened, and I just want her with me for whatever crazy stuff happens next."

I got up and hugged Georgie. "I'm so happy for you guys." I pushed back and lowered my voice. "Any news on Adele?"

Georgie shook her head. "They're sure that she wasn't killed in the City. But no one has seen her. They thought her shuttle was headed for Buckley, but it went off the radar somewhere over the Gulf. They're sure it didn't crash, because they've combed the Gulf for wreckage. I think they had some sort of signal jammer that allowed them to go off the radar."

I sighed. "So, the tech is lost, then." Ginger hadn't been able to recover any useful information on the exact techniques used to capture Goliath, or to create tornados. There had been some kind of fail-safe built into the programming that when we shut down the storm, it wiped the data clean. Only Ashton would have been able to recreate it. And he was dead.

Trig and Gretchen came out of the house with trays of snacks, teasing and laughing with each other. Trig set his tray down, then took Gretchen's from her. She gave him a playful frown and punched him in the arm. He grabbed her hand and pulled her close, telling her something. Her frown melted into a bashful smile, and she leaned forward and gave him a quick peck on the lips. I shook my head.

Dasha snorted. "I can't get over it, either. But they really bonded when you were missing."

My heart twisted. "Dash, I'm so sorry."

She gave my foot a gentle kick. "No more sorries. You're here, and so is your dad. That is all that matters."

I swallowed hard. "Well, that and the trial next week."

Dad, Mom, and the Storm Chasers had all been summoned as witnesses in Chip's trial. He was being charged with kidnapping, environmental terrorism, and racketeering. The trial had already become very public, and we all had to go on the stand to testify against him. I was glad, but I was also ready for the whole thing to be over.

Dasha grinned. "You'll have lots of fun information to give during freshman orientation, when they ask what you did all summer." She walked away to join Gretchen and Rosalie, who were hanging out with Trig.

It was more than a graduation party. It was a reunion, with everyone from the Storm Chasers there. Jack and Miri sat with Ginger and Silas at our patio table. Even Sybil had come, although I could tell she was sad to have missed going into the Eye. Almost every one of my teachers had come through, along with the principal of my school. He gave me my diploma, even though I technically didn't finish the last three weeks.

I was thankful that Mason had not come. I didn't invite him, but I didn't invite a lot of my classmates who had shown up. I didn't mind them, but I did not need or want to see Mason. I was pretty sure Dasha told him to stay away.

"Whoa, hey guys! Come here!" Jack waved wildly at Luca and me. I glanced at Luca and shrugged, and we made our way over to the patio table. They were huddled around Ginger's tech pad.

Miri's eye's twinkled as we got there. "Have you seen this?"

Ginger pushed a few buttons, and cast the show from her pad to the screen on the side of the house. The party quieted down as the music switched to the interview on the screen.

"Is this Secrets from the Eye?" Luca asked.

It didn't take long for the news apps to latch on to what had happened in the City. They were slowly getting information from the few residents who were willing to talk to them. Decades of conditioning made the citizens of the Eye tight-lipped about everything, including who was in charge down there. The government tried to offer them assistance on relocation or rebuilding, but so far not many were taking them up on it. Other hurricane communities, like Ousely, were very vocal about their experiences, though, and the public ate it up. And, of course, the shows were quick to make up theories about whatever they couldn't get answers about. We Storm Chasers were addicted to the Secrets from the Eye show.

Georgie gasped. "It's Adele!"

I leaned in to get a better look. The woman on the couch next to the host kind of looked like Adele. Her hair was dark brown and cut very short. There was something about her nose, too, that wasn't quite right. She was dressed like someone who liked hiking in the mountains, not like the breezy beach woman from Florida.

"Yes, I'm Runa. I ran the Med Centers in the Eye."

I looked at Georgie. "I know that's not Runa. But are you sure it's Adele?"

Georgie's face was pale. "I know it's Adele. She must have gone into a cosmetic med chamber. We didn't use them in the City, but I knew they existed. Wherever she went, there must have been one."

"Runa is with us today to share some of the wonderful medical advances she had developed in the Eye," the host explained. "Stay with us to the end to find out how this technology could be coming to your family very soon, for a very reasonable price."

I shook my head and turned to Luca. "So, that was her plan. Get the med tech out into the world, so she could sell it."

Silas sighed. "Well? Do we need to do something about this?"

"I'm not sure what we could do," Ginger said. "I mean, I guess the tech belongs to her. She can do what she wants with it."

Hugh put his arm around Georgie. "We don't need to do anything today. Right?"

Georgie gave him a soft smile and nodded.

I took a deep breath in through my nose and closed my eyes. Whatever her game was, it didn't matter. For me, it was over. My dad was home, and I could focus on the next part of my life, which was figuring out the next part of my life. For the first time I could remember, I didn't mind that I didn't know what was coming next.

The skies were clear and would be for a long time.

Acknowledgements

A special thank you to my super fans, Dad, Megan, Jaclyn, and Bria. This story would not exist without your encouragement and ideas.

I'm also forever grateful to Mindy, Kara, and Lori. Your insights are invaluable.

About the Author

Victoria lives at the foot of the Rocky Mountains in Colorado with her husband, her three girls, and her unemployed housecat. She is a a full-fledged homebody, a so-so housekeeper, a mediocre musician, an amateur weather nerd, and has dreamed of writing her whole life.

ALSO BY VICTORIA KIMBLE

YA Thrillers
The Hurricane Trilogy
The Hurricane Keeper
The Eyewall Seeker

Contemporary YA Fiction
The Main Dish

Faith- Based Middle Grade Contemporary Fiction
The Choir Girls Series
Soprano Trouble
Alto Secrets
Harmony Blues
Solo Disaster

Writing Prompts for Humans
Writing Prompts for the Hungry
Writing Prompts for the Animal Lover
Writing Prompts for the Nerds, Geeks, & Dorks
Writing Prompts for the Outdoorsy
Writing Prompts for the Suspicious